LOVERS IN LONDON

Lanthia was thinking again about her dream man who always rode beside her in the woods and instinctively the thought made her yearn for fresh air and so she ran to the window.

She looked out onto Portland Place.

At the same time she was still feeling as if she was riding beneath the trees in the woods at home.

The sun was percolating through their broad leaves and someone was riding beside her.

Someone who understood that she was listening to the goblins working deep in the ground.

Someone who could see the nymphs hiding behind the trunks of the trees.

How could she explain to the Marquis or to anyone else the strange feelings she then harboured within her.

Nor would they understand that she was talking to the invisible man beside her, who felt the same as she did about everything.

'How can I marry *anyone*,' she asked herself, 'if I am always thinking about someone else, even though he is invisible.'

THE BARBARA CARTLAND PINK COLLECTION

Titles in this series

LOVERS IN LONDON

BARBARA CARTLAND

Barbaracartland.com Ltd

THE BARBARA CARTLAND PINK COLLECTION

Barbara Cartland was the most prolific bestselling author in the history of the world. She was frequently in the Guinness Book of Records for writing more books in a year than any other living author. In fact her most amazing literary feat was when her publishers asked for more Barbara Cartland romances, she doubled her output from 10 books a year to over 20 books a year, when she was 77.

She went on writing continuously at this rate for 20 years and wrote her last book at the age of 97, thus completing 400 books between the ages of 77 and 97.

Her publishers finally could not keep up with this phenomenal output, so at her death she left 160 unpublished manuscripts, something again that no other author has ever achieved.

Now the exciting news is that these 160 original unpublished Barbara Cartland books are already being published and by Barbaracartland.com exclusively on the internet, as the international web is the best possible way of reaching so many Barbara Cartland readers around the world.

The 160 books are published monthly and will be numbered in sequence.

The series is called the Pink Collection as a tribute to Barbara Cartland whose favourite colour was pink and it became very much her trademark over the years.

The Barbara Cartland Pink Collection is published only on the internet. Log on to www.barbaracartland.com to find out how you can purchase the books monthly as they are published, and take out a subscription that will ensure that all subsequent editions are delivered to you by mail order to your home.

NEW

Barbaracartland.com is proud to announce the publication of ten new Audio Books for the first time as CDs. They are favourite Barbara Cartland stories read by well-known actors and actresses and each story extends to 4 or 5 CDs. The Audio Books are as follows :

The Patient Bridegroom	The Passion and the Flower
A Challenge of Hearts	Little White Doves of Love
A Train to Love	The Prince and the Pekinese
The Unbroken Dream	A King in Love
The Cruel Count	A Sign of Love

More Audio Books will be published in the future and the above titles can be purchased by logging on to the website www.barbaracartland.com or please write to the address below.

If you do not have access to a computer, you can write for information about the Barbara Cartland Pink Collection and the Barbara Cartland Audio Books to the following address:

Barbara Cartland.com Ltd., Camfield Place, Hatfield, Hertfordshire AL9 6JE, United Kingdom.

Telephone: +44 (0)1707 642629
Fax: +44 (0)1707 663041

THE LATE DAME BARBARA CARTLAND

Barbara Cartland who sadly died in May 2000 at the age of nearly 99 was the world's most famous romantic novelist who wrote 723 books in her lifetime with worldwide sales of over 1 billion copies and her books were translated into 36 different languages.

As well as romantic novels, she wrote historical biographies, 6 autobiographies, theatrical plays, books of advice on life, love, vitamins and cookery. She also found time to be a political speaker and television and radio personality.

She wrote her first book at the age of 21 and this was called *Jigsaw*. It became an immediate bestseller and sold 100,000 copies in hardback and was translated into 6 different languages. She wrote continuously throughout her life, writing bestsellers for an astonishing 76 years. Her books have always been immensely popular in the United States, where in 1976 her current books were at numbers 1 & 2 in the B. Dalton bestsellers list, a feat never achieved before or since by any author.

Barbara Cartland became a legend in her own lifetime and will be best remembered for her wonderful romantic novels, so loved by her millions of readers throughout the world.

Her books will always be treasured for their moral message, her pure and innocent heroines, her good looking and dashing heroes and above all her belief that the power of love is more important than anything else in everyone's life.

" London for me has always been the most romantic city in the world and I really did fall in love in Berkeley Square!"

Barbara Cartland

CHAPTER ONE
1880

Lanthia was riding alone through the woods as she did every morning.

She was thinking that nothing in the universe could be lovelier than the sunshine streaming through the spring leaves and turning them to gold.

She was telling herself a story, because whenever she rode into the woods stories just seemed to flow into her mind.

As she often said to her father, she had travelled the world from the books in his library and the stories he told her.

"They all seem so true and real, Papa," she had told him over and over again.

Her father had laughed.

Sir Philip Grenville had been very much an ardent traveller ever since he was a very young man, but now he was content to stay at home in the country.

He wrote about his experiences rather than taking part any more.

To Lanthia, ever since she had been small, the huge library with so many books overflowing into almost every other room in the house created many fairy tales in which she herself always played a vital part.

She envisaged herself climbing up the Himalayas as her father had tried to do, or travelling for endless miles over deserted countryside to Tibet and finding a monastery perched on the side of a cliff where no European had ever set foot.

In all her dreams she was always accompanied by someone special who understood what she was thinking and who enjoyed the adventure of discovering a new world as much as she enjoyed it herself.

She dreamed, as she was travelling up the Nile or the Amazon, that she instructed her invisible companion.

At other times he instructed her.

She had always been a lonely child.

At her birth her mother was thirty-nine years old.

When the Honourable Elizabeth Ford had married Philip Grenville – he had not by then come into the family Baronetcy – they had a son and heir after they had been married for only a year.

But because Philip Grenville wanted to travel the world and his wife always went with him, there were no more children.

However, they did accept that their family was now complete and had given up hoping that there might be any more.

Unexpectedly, as an 'afterthought,' as someone had commented, Lanthia arrived.

Her parents were so thrilled and delighted as if the fates had given them a special gift when they were least expecting it.

Lanthia herself had always looked as if she had stepped straight out of a fairy story.

Sir Philip was prouder of his daughter than of the books he wrote or of his vast library and he spent a great deal of time telling her stories, which fascinated her until she began to feel that she was living in them rather than just hearing them.

Now she was riding through the woods which were part of her father's country estate.

She was blissfully imagining that she was riding in the hot sun in India towards a magnificent Palace, where she was to stay with the Maharajah.

India was very often in her thoughts because that was where her brother, David, was presently stationed. He was serving as *aide-de-camp* to the Viceroy.

He did not write to her very often, but when he did, it made Lanthia feel she was exploring India herself.

In her mind she travelled from the Viceregal Lodge in Calcutta to the North-West Frontier where many hostile tribesmen lurked behind every rock and bush and she could visualise all too well the dangers she would be facing.

David had told her when he was last at home for a short leave how afraid they all felt about infiltration by the Russians.

She could almost see the Cossacks riding across the desolate plains towards India, which was then considered the most magnificent jewel in the British Crown.

But the Czar himself and the Cossacks who served him were determined it should sooner or later be in their hands.

"We have to be always on our guard," David told his sister, who listened to him wide-eyed.

"The Russians infiltrate," he went on, "amongst the local tribesmen and incite them to rebel against us. They intrigue with the ordinary Indians everywhere and we are never sure what mischief they are plotting until the trouble actually strikes us."

He also told her how beautiful the Palaces were and how India itself was so enchanting.

When he returned to his duties Lanthia felt as if she was still with him.

She was, in her mind, living in India amongst its smiling people, its exquisite monuments and its burning sun.

Now the sunshine was only slightly warm on her soft cheeks, but it glittered on her fair hair as she was not wearing a hat.

It was so much easier when she rode alone just to jump onto a horse. Why bother about jackets, hats and of course gloves, which every lady who rode was expected to wear?

Her fine black stallion was called Jupiter after the King of the Gods and she loved him best after her parents.

He seemed to understand everything she was saying when she talked to him. The grooms had told her and she knew it was true, that when it was her regular time to come to the stables, Jupiter was always waiting at the door of his stall listening for her footsteps.

Now as they moved slowly over the moss-covered paths in the woods, Lanthia was talking to him,

"Today, Jupiter, we have been riding over the hot plains of India and were very grateful for any shelter we could find from the sun."

She thought Jupiter was listening and continued,

"Somewhere in a large and grand Palace we shall learn a secret which will send us off tomorrow on another journey of discovery. It will send us into a very dangerous situation from which we will extract ourselves at the very last moment only by what would seem a miracle!"

As she was talking to Jupiter, she could see it all happening and she knew that only the Gods could save her from destruction.

At that moment in her story, the wood came to an end and she saw her home ahead of her.

It was a very attractive house which had been in the

Grenville family for more than two hundred years and in fact it had originally been built by a Grenville, one of the first Baronets ever created by King James I.

Over the centuries the house had been considerably extended and Sir Philip's great-grandfather had spent a great deal of money on it.

He had added, besides his large collection of books, many modern comforts which had not been available to his ancestors.

There were a large number of trees surrounding the house and the garden was the particular pride and delight of Lanthia's mother.

When she had first married her husband, they had not troubled about having a home of their own as they were too busy travelling round the world.

When they were in England they often stayed with his father and mother, who were only too delighted to have them. It was they who had looked after David when he was born.

As soon as Elizabeth was strong enough to leave the infant boy, her husband was eager to set off again on another journey of discovery.

This time it was to Africa as he had wanted to find a tribe which people knew very little about, yet professed an ancient history of its own which had never been written down on paper.

It was only now, as Sir Philip was growing old and so was his wife, although she did not like to admit it, that they were content to stay at home.

"I want so much to go exploring with you, Papa," Lanthia had said almost as soon as she could talk.

To keep her happy her parents had taken her with them on some short journeys to the Continent.

By the time she was old enough to fully understand what it meant to explore unknown parts of the world, she found that her father and mother now wished to remain in Huntingdonshire.

There was not much to amuse Lanthia at home as she grew up and this made her all the more interested in the books she could read and the stories her father told her.

She now rode slowly up the drive with its ancient oak trees lining each side like sentinels.

She had no idea that she really looked as if she had stepped out of a storybook herself and was not an ordinary human being.

Lanthia was a very lovely young girl, but it was not just her looks. There was something ethereal about her that was intangible and it made everyone who met her feel drawn towards her as by a magnet.

It was not exactly what she said, but it was as if she was speaking to everyone around her through an aura that radiated from her soul.

Sir Philip had once said to his wife,

"When I am with Lanthia, I always feel as if she is a veritable Goddess who has graciously come down to us from Mount Olympus and might vanish at any moment!"

Lady Grenville had laughed.

"I know exactly what you mean, my dearest," she replied, "and it is your fault. The world you have created for her is more real than the actual world she lives in!"

Now as Lanthia looked at her home, she thought how beautiful the ancient brick was and that it had a life of its own because of the many years it had existed.

She was daydreaming about the many people who had passed through its doors and felt they had all left an impression she could feel in the atmosphere of the house.

There had been soldiers and statesmen, rakes and roués, and politicians of every persuasion who had been of great service to the country.

They had all come and they had all gone.

Sometimes Lanthia felt as if they were still there, watching over their namesake and preparing the way for those who would follow in the future.

'That will be David,' ruminated Lanthia, 'and it is time he married and produced an heir who will be the tenth Baronet when he dies.'

She rode into the stables and one of the boys came out to take charge of Jupiter.

"Did you 'ave a nice ride, miss?" he asked.

"It was lovely, as it always is and if I can, I will go riding again this evening."

The stable boy grinned as if he knew without being told.

Lanthia loved to be riding Jupiter when the sun was beginning to sink in the sky and the shadows were growing a little longer.

It was then that everything seemed mysterious.

There was a sudden hush over the world and she felt that she was nearer to the unknown.

It was then that the best stories would come to her mind and she found them completely realistic. She could almost see them all happening as well as feel them in her heart.

*

As she walked back to the house, she wondered if her father would do anything with her this afternoon.

Sometimes he would place aside the book he was writing and say he must inspect something on the estate or visit one of the tenant farmers.

Or perhaps he would just ride with her for the sheer joy of doing so.

Because the possibility of his riding with her was so exciting, she hurried into the hall.

She wondered if she should now go to her father's study, but he disliked being disturbed if he was busy.

It was, however, nearly time for luncheon and one thing her mother always insisted upon was that Sir Philip should take proper meals at proper times.

She would never permit him to concentrate on his book to the extent that it might affect his health, which was something he had done in the past, working flat out all day with nothing to eat or drink.

It was simply because he was so engrossed with his writing that he felt he could not bear to break the spell it cast over him.

Now that he was getting on for sixty his wife was insistent that he should take better care of himself.

Because he loved her so much, he did whatever she asked of him.

'It is five minutes to one,' thought Lanthia. 'He will not be annoyed if I disturb him now.'

She ran along the passage.

Sir Philip's study was next to the library so that he did not have far to go when he needed a book to help with his research.

Very softly Lanthia opened the door.

Then she saw that her father was not alone but her mother was with him.

She entered and Sir Philip exclaimed,

"Oh, there you are Lanthia! Your mother was just talking about you."

"I have been riding, Papa, and I am hoping that you might ride with me this afternoon."

Sir Philip smiled at her.

"Your mother has something to tell you."

Lanthia looked towards her mother expectantly.

"We have received an invitation, darling," she said, "to a ball which is being given by the Lord Lieutenant. It will be a most auspicious occasion because he is holding it for the Empress of Austria, who you will remember stayed at his house for a short while last year."

"She did so because she specially wanted to see his horses," added Lanthia. "You know what a fine stable the Earl has and apparently she was entranced with them."

"Well she is coming again and he is giving a ball for her this time. As it is such an important event for the County, darling, you should look your best and you will need a new gown."

"I have hardly worn the last one you bought for me, Mama. Being in mourning for Grandpapa, there have been so few times when I could wear it."

"I know that, Lanthia, but most of the County have seen it and I want you to look your most beautiful when we attend this ball in three weeks time."

She spoke in a way which made Lanthia realise that her mother had made a decision about something.

She waited patiently to hear what it was.

"I have been talking to your father," Lady Grenville said at last, "and as it is impossible for me to do very much at the moment until my knee is better, you will have to go to London without me."

"To *London*!" cried Lanthia in astonishment.

Her mother smiled.

"When I said a new gown, I meant one that is really fashionable and up-to-date and that of course means Bond Street."

"Are we not all going to London?" asked Lanthia looking at her father to see what he thought.

"I am afraid that is quite impossible, darling. This tiresome rheumatism I am suffering from would make it impossible for me to walk from shop to shop, as we should undoubtedly have to do to find just what we need and you know your father is in the middle of his new book and, of course, will not be drawn away from it."

"Or from you," Sir Philip came in with a smile.

He adored his wife as she adored him.

Lanthia knew that it would be quite impossible to talk her father into coming to London if her mother was staying at home.

"What am I to do?" she implored her mother.

"We have just been talking it over and we know that Mrs. Blossom would be only too willing to travel to London with you as your chaperone."

"Mrs. Blossom!" she repeated without very much enthusiasm.

"I know, my dearest, she is rather dull, but, as I was saying to your father, all our relations seem to be in the country at the moment and your Aunt Mary told me quite specifically last time she was here that she had no intention of opening their London house in Belgrave Square until the autumn."

"Then where will I and Mrs. Blossom stay?"

"Your Papa and I are quite certain that you will be well looked after and quite safe at *The Langham*."

"*The Langham*!" cried Lanthia. "Oh, I would love that!"

She had been to *The Langham* once with her father and mother when she was a young girl and thought it was a fascinating hotel.

The Langham was one of London's newest hotels and its owners claimed that it was the largest building in England when it was opened in 1865 by the young Prince of Wales. The hotel boasted no less than five hundred bedrooms, dwarfing their rivals such as *Claridges* and *The Grosvenor*.

When Sir Philip had to go to London to see about his books being published or for any other reason, he and his wife always stayed at *The Langham*.

Their last visit had been two years ago, but they did not take Lanthia with them as she was so occupied with her governesses.

Lanthia believed then, as she did now, that they had actually wanted to be on their own and she knew that *The Langham* held so many happy memories for them.

She herself could remember being very impressed by the hotel and some of the stories her father had told her about people who stayed there had remained in her mind.

She remembered now him telling her on his return home all about the romantic novelist, Louisa Ramée, who lived in *The Langham*.

Lanthia knew that Louisa Ramée was known to the world by her pen name, 'Ouida,' which originated from her own attempts as a baby to pronounce 'Louisa'.

Since her father had met Ouida, he had bought her novels – she published one nearly every year. And she could remember her mother reading various passages aloud so that her father could laugh at them with her.

Last year when her father had just bought the latest novel by Ouida, he had told Lanthia what a strange woman she was.

"She is different from anyone else I have ever met," he had said.

"Why does she live in a hotel, Papa?"

"I have really no idea," he answered. "Apparently she first stayed at *The Langham* when she was twenty-eight and has lived there ever since. They told us when we were staying there how she receives her visitors in bed and it is where she writes all her books!"

"In bed, Papa! What a funny thing to do!"

"She is indeed a very strange woman. She likes to work by the light of candles and has black velvet curtains drawn over the windows to keep out the daylight."

"I hear that she is always surrounded by masses of flowers," Lady Grenville had chimed in, "and they are all purple. Her enormous bed is in the middle of the room and she sits up writing with a quill pen onto sheets of violet-coloured writing paper."

Lanthia had laughed loudly at the time, thinking it all sounded ridiculous.

Now she wondered if she stayed at *The Langham*, whether she would be able to meet the famous authoress.

"Do you think you could give me an introduction to her, Papa?" she asked.

"I doubt if she is still resident at the hotel, my dear, and even if she is, I do not think she would be very anxious to meet you."

"Why ever not?"

"Because," her mother answered, "Ouida prefers men to women. I am told that her parties at the hotel were always attended by handsome Army Officers and very few women were invited."

It certainly had seemed very strange at the time and now she remembered the story and it made her feel that it would be exciting to be even staying in the same hotel as such a weird and unaccountable authoress.

"When do you think I should go, Mama?"

"We shall have to ask Mrs. Blossom when it suits her, darling, but she has always told me she would be only too willing to do anything I request and I know she enjoys going to London when she has the chance."

Mrs. Blossom was the only daughter of the Bishop of Bristol and she had married for the first and only time to a sailor when she was long past her girlhood.

He had retired to live in a house he had inherited from his uncle in Huntingdonshire where he had died after five years of marriage without having any children.

Broken-hearted, Mrs. Blossom had been left alone which she had found dull and was miserable without her husband.

She had therefore begged Lady Grenville to find her something to do, but it was not an easy task.

However, she had managed to make Mrs. Blossom interested in a number of charities in the County and they were only too delighted to receive her attention and help.

There was a nearby orphanage where she had been persuaded to teach the girls how to paint in watercolours at which Mrs. Blossom was actually quite an expert.

She was exceedingly grateful to Lady Grenville for making her life much more interesting than it would have been otherwise.

Lanthia knew all too well that if her mother asked Mrs. Blossom to take her to London, she would be only too willing to do so.

"Very well, Mama, you ask Mrs. Blossom. But I do not want to stay away from you and Papa for any longer than I have to."

"Just long enough to buy some really pretty dresses and a special gown for the ball."

"I hope I shall be able to choose something you will like," said Lanthia doubtfully. "It would be disastrous if I spent a great deal of money and you and Papa thought my choice was hideous."

Lady Grenville laughed.

"I have always considered your taste impeccable, darling, and you know exactly the sort of white gown I would like you to wear. Remember you are a *debutante*, even though you have never had a Season in London."

"That was poor old Grandpapa's fault for dying last year when I should have been in London with you. Now at nearly nineteen I am almost old enough to be a Dowager!"

Her mother laughed again.

"Papa and I are now planning that we will take you to Ascot and, of course, there will be plenty of balls then."

Lanthia gave a cry of delight.

"Oh, Mama! You did not tell me!"

"It was to be a surprise, but Ascot is just one reason why I really want you to start choosing pretty gowns now, because unless my leg gets better quickly we shall not have much time before we will all have to go to London."

"For you and Papa to enjoy the racing at Ascot and for me to go to parties every night!"

Lanthia kissed her mother.

"You did not tell me all this, Mama, but it sounds so exciting."

"I am only frightened that I will just not be well enough. When the doctor called this morning he said he is quite certain that I will be my old self by next month, but I am to do as little as possible until then."

"Of course you must do exactly as he says. Oh, Mama, it will be the most wonderful thing that has ever happened to me to go to Ascot with you and Papa! I only wish we were entering a horse for the Gold Cup."

Sir Philip chuckled.

"That is something I definitely cannot afford, even though I would enjoy owning a racehorse!"

"Perhaps if your book is a huge success, Papa, next year you may be able to buy one horse which is so good that we can run him at Ascot."

"It is just a case of 'if wishes were horses, beggars might ride', Lanthia, you are not to try to tempt me to wild extravagance, as I am saving up for your wedding when you have one."

"That will be a long, long time away, Papa. I have no wish to marry anyone."

That was not exactly true.

In her dreams she fervently believed she had a very special man in her life who was completely invisible, but he was exploring the world with her.

She had always thought in her heart of hearts that he was the man she would eventually marry.

But she had no intention of marrying anyone unless she was as much in love with him as her mother was with her father and he loved her in the same way.

Lanthia had grown up in a house filled with love.

From all the books she had read she had been made vividly aware of the power of love and she was brought up to appreciate that it was something that men and women had always sought since the beginning of time.

So many events had occurred entirely as a result of love – misery, crime, war, cruelty and blissful happiness, because two people had found each other.

It was in the books about Greece that Lanthia had read about how real love began.

The ancient Greeks themselves fervently believed that when God first created a human being, he just made a man.

But the man was lonely all by himself.

God therefore cut him in half making one half the woman and the other half the man.

It was the woman who was sweet, gentle, loving and inspiring and equally it was the man who was strong, protective, masculine and adventurous.

Together they made one complete person, just as they had been before he was divided into two.

'That is what I am looking for,' Lanthia had often told herself.

That particular fancy crept into her dreams and the stories she lived in as she went riding.

She was, however, well aware that her mother had hoped that she and the Lord Lieutenant's eldest son would be attracted to each other.

He was really quite a nice young man and Lanthia had known him since they were children, but he was not particularly interested in her and if she was honest, she found him rather dull.

He was certainly not the hero of her dreams or her imagination.

She had no desire to climb up the highest mountain with him or go down deep into the darkness of the earth.

'The man I marry will have to be *different*, very different,' she told herself many times.

So far she had not met him, nor had there been any occasion when she might have done.

Her mother's father, Lord Leamsford, had died last year at a very inconvenient time and his unexpected death had postponed her 'coming out' as a *debutante*.

It had not worried Lanthia particularly, but it had upset her parents' plans for her introduction to Society.

There was nothing they could do but stay quietly in the country and entertain in only a small way.

Queen Victoria had set down the rules of mourning by excessively overdoing it for Prince Albert who had died in 1861. She was still, almost twenty years later, draped in black crêpe and refusing to attend all functions which were just for amusement.

It was generally accepted that anyone who tried to shorten their period of mourning for a relative was committing a Social error.

The unwritten laws of Society were very strict.

Deep black for six months, purple and anything that could be considered half-mourning for the next six months.

It was the young girls who suffered most.

A *debutante*, once she had been presented at Court, was invited to attend all the glamorous balls, receptions and garden parties which took place in the Social world.

It was impossible to attend any of these if one was dressed in black.

Only the smaller and less important occasions were permissible when one was in half-mourning.

"It is just not fair," Lanthia had said to her mother several times.

"There is nothing we can do about it, dearest, and as you well know, everyone is much too frightened of the Queen to break the rules."

But now she was free.

Lanthia knew that her mother was perfectly right in saying she should buy new clothes, especially if they were to be in London for Ascot and she was to attend the ball given by the Lord Lieutenant.

"I want you to look your very best, my dearest," Sir Philip had said. "But do not bankrupt me completely!"

"I will try not to, Papa. At the same time I want to be a good advertisement for your books. If I was to look tatty, people may assume that nothing you have written is worth reading!"

She was only teasing him and he laughed before he answered,

"You are quite right. If I have to rely on you to sell my books, then you must certainly come out in frills and furbelows so that you will be the belle of the ball!"

He looked at his wife as he spoke, knowing she was certain that was just what Lanthia would most certainly be.

There was no doubt she was very lovely.

In fact he had said to her moments before Lanthia returned from riding, she was so beautiful that at times he could hardly believe she was real.

They both thought it would be a mistake to praise Lanthia to her face, but both Sir Philip and his wife were convinced that once Lanthia appeared in the Social world, she would be a sensation.

"I often wonder, darling," Lady Grenville had said, "how we managed to produce anything quite so *exquisite* as Lanthia."

"I know the answer to that," he replied, "because, my precious wife, I love you with all my heart and soul and I believe you feel the same about me."

"You know I did when I first married you, Philip, and I have loved you more every year since."

Sir Philip bent down to kiss her.

"I worship you," he said, "and we are the luckiest couple in the whole world because, unlike many others, we have found what we were seeking. It is ours now and for ever."

Lady Grenville had looked up at him adoringly.

He was still very handsome.

She had thought when she first saw him that he was the best-looking man she could ever have dreamt about.

She herself had been the most admired *debutante* of her Season.

Sir Philip was surely right when he said that her beauty had indeed deepened year by year because she was so happy. Even now she was so attractive that men always seemed to surround her wherever she went.

"I have often felt," Sir Philip had said once, "that I might have been forced to fight a thousand duels to prevent you from being taken away from me!"

"Do you think I would ever have left you?" his wife asked softly. "I knew the moment I first saw you that you were the man of my dreams. I was only terrified that you would disappear on one of your expeditions and I would never see you again!"

Actually it had been a question of love at first sight and there had been no chance of either of them escaping from the other.

Their son had been a most adorable baby and had grown up to be a very good-looking young man.

But Lanthia was really exceptional.

As he looked at her now, Sir Philip wondered what would happen to her in the future.

Perhaps it was a mistake to let her go to London, even to buy a few clothes. Then he told himself he was being unnecessarily anxious.

She would only be away for three or four days.

Mrs. Blossom could be relied on to look after her.

'I expect I am prejudiced,' Sir Philip thought, 'but she does look like Aphrodite and what man in his own way is not seeking the Goddess of Love?'

CHAPTER TWO

Lanthia and Mrs. Blossom travelled to London by train and when they reached the terminus they engaged a Hackney Carriage to drive to *The Langham*.

The front door boasted a most impressive portico and they were greeted by the hotel manager who welcomed Lanthia most effusively.

"I received a letter from Sir Philip, Miss Grenville," he said, "and I cannot tell you how delighted I am that you have returned to *The Langham* after all these years."

"I have certainly grown since I was here last," she smiled, "and I see the hotel is looking magnificent!"

"That is what we hoped you would think and that you will be comfortable with us," the manager replied.

Lanthia introduced Mrs. Blossom and told him that her father was the Bishop of Bristol, who had frequently stayed at *The Langham*.

The Manager made a few complimentary remarks about the Bishop, Sir Philip and Lanthia's mother before he escorted them upstairs.

They went up to the second floor in a hydraulically operated lift which was widely known as a 'rising room' and as they did so the manager apologetically explained to them that the hotel was very full.

He could therefore only give Lanthia one bedroom with a sitting room, the other bedroom being further down the corridor.

"I can assure you, Miss Grenville, that the moment a guest moves from the other side of the sitting room, I will of course move Mrs. Blossom into that room."

"Perhaps Mrs. Blossom would like to stay in the bedroom with the sitting room," suggested Lanthia.

"No, of course not," she responded. "You may be having visitors. Your mother has told me she was writing to several friends to see if they are in London and I shall be perfectly happy as long as I have a comfortable bed."

"I can definitely promise you that," the manager assured her.

When they came out of the lift they walked down a long, wide corridor.

Lanthia remembered her father telling her that the hotel corridors were just broad enough for two ladies in crinolines – which were very much the fashion when the hotel was built – to walk side by side. Now the corridors were furnished with sofas and chairs and were as luxurious as every other part of the hotel.

Lady Grenville had told Lanthia that there had been many recent improvements.

For one example the columns, which had originally been brown were now painted white to go with the rest of the decorations in which white, scarlet and gold prevailed.

"We are now most up-to-date," the manager was saying proudly as they walked along the corridor. "You will notice this evening, Miss Grenville, that the entrance and the courtyard are now lit by electricity."

Lanthia confirmed that she was impressed and then she asked what she had been longing to know.

"Is Madame Ouida still living here in the hotel?"

"Yes, indeed she is," replied the manager, "but at the moment she has left on a visit to Paris. We expect her back in a month or so."

"My father met her when he was staying here."

The manager smiled.

"I think there is no one of any importance who has not been received by Madame at one time or another in her bedroom!"

He paused as if he was very carefully choosing his words, before he added,

"In fact one of her visitors was staying here only a week ago and that was Mr. Richard Burton."

Lanthia gave a little cry of excitement.

"Oh, I do wish I had seen him! He has always been one of the most interesting people I have ever read about and I would like more than anything else to meet him!"

She was thinking as she spoke of what she had read about him in one of her father's books.

He had described in detail Richard Burton's 'dark Arabic face and his questing panther eyes.'

What really interested her so much was that he was the world's greatest living explorer and she had followed his brilliant adventures with the same excitement that she had followed her father's.

Richard Burton was one of the few men alive who had reached the inner sanctuary at Mecca and he had seen what few other infidels had ever lived to describe.

Lanthia learnt that he spoke twenty-eight languages and many strange Oriental dialects.

'If only he was staying here at *The Langham* now,' she thought, 'how wonderful it would have been to see him and perhaps even speak with him.'

As if the manager could sense her disappointment he said,

"I am sure Mr. Burton will come back here many times and I can only hope, Miss Grenville, you are with us when he arrives."

"I really hope so too!"

To soften Lanthia's disappointment, he told her that the Prime Minister had been in for dinner only last week.

'He is a poor substitute,' she thought, 'for Richard Burton!'

However, she forced herself to sound just a little bit enthusiastic about the Prime Minister.

When they reached her sitting room, she found it to be quite small but comfortable and her bedroom opening out of it was pretty with a four-poster bed.

The manager was still making abject apologies for not being able to provide what they had wanted.

He showed Mrs. Blossom the other bedroom which was only a few yards away.

"I will certainly be perfectly comfortable here," she stated firmly.

By this time the porters had brought their luggage upstairs and deposited it in the bedrooms.

Lanthia tipped them, giving the sum her father had advised her to do and as they seemed very grateful, they obviously thought it was generous.

"Now if there is anything you should require, Miss Grenville," the manager was saying, "or if you have any complaints, please let me know. I know your father would want me to look after you and to make your visit to *The Langham* a happy and memorable one."

"I am sure that is just what it will be and thank you so much."

When the manager had left them she ordered tea, knowing that was what Mrs. Blossom would need.

She then unpacked the dresses she had brought with her and hung them up in the wardrobe.

"We had better start out early tomorrow morning to find all the gowns I require," she now suggested to Mrs. Blossom. "Otherwise I feel we shall have to stay here for weeks and I am sure it is a very expensive hotel."

"I am afraid it's true," agreed Mrs. Blossom, "but I know your father and mother would not like you to stay in any hotel which indeed might be a bit cheaper, but not so respectable!"

"I doubt if we shall have time to do anything else but shop," sighed Lanthia, "and we will be so tired when we return to the hotel, we will just want to rest."

Mrs. Blossom agreed with her at once, but Lanthia could not help feeling the prospect sounded rather dull.

She therefore insisted that they went downstairs for dinner as it would be more fun than having it brought up to the sitting room.

Lanthia changed into one of her simplest evening frocks and once downstairs she was very delighted with the elegance of everything she saw.

There were marble pillars, fine silk hangings, hand-printed wallpapers and Persian tapestry carpets which her mother had told her were outstanding for a London hotel.

It was all very grand.

She felt as if it was a stage-set designed particularly for all the important people who stayed there.

It seemed as if everything had come straight out of a story book.

As Mrs. Blossom was tired after the journey, they went back upstairs as soon as they had finished dinner.

Having said goodnight to Lanthia, she hurried to her own bedroom.

Lanthia walked to the window and stood for a long time looking down at Portland Place.

It was not a very busy street, but there were smart carriages drawn by well-bred horses passing down it.

She started imagine they were all taking glamorous ladies out to dinner.

It was so long since she had last been to London and now she was here she felt she had just stepped into a different world.

It was all more dreamlike than reality.

'I wish Papa was with me,' mused Lanthia. 'I am sure he would have new stories to tell me about everything I see.'

It was consoling that in a month they would all be coming to London and then it would be really exciting with all the balls, parties and the racing at Ascot.

'I am lucky, so very lucky,' she told herself.

At the same time she could not help wishing that tonight she was being taken to a ball in one of the carriages passing below her window.

And that there would be plenty of young men there anxious to dance with her!

This was what she might have been doing last year, but by being in mourning a whole year had been wasted.

'I suppose I should not think of it like that. I have learned so much this past year from Papa and all his books and of course the woods have told me things which I would never have learned in the noise and hurry of a big city.'

She undressed and climbed into her bed, but it was a long time before she fell asleep.

*

The next morning she and Mrs. Blossom had their breakfast at eight o'clock and before the clock had struck nine they had left the hotel.

The many shops in Bond Street were as alluring as her mother had said they would be, but she was determined not to rush into buying anything too quickly as she might easily find something more attractive a bit later and regret her first purchase.

They inspected the gowns in several shops and then they would make a decision as to which was the prettiest and most becoming.

Lanthia had no idea that every dress she would try on seemed as if it had been specially designed for her and made her look even more beautiful than ever.

Up to now she had received very few compliments and she was very unselfconscious.

She seldom thought about her own appearance, but she did love bright colours and beauty wherever she found them.

She was entranced with the amusing little hats that were now the fashion and trimmed with flowers or a single feather they made her look very smart and up-to-date.

"Which shall I buy?" she asked Mrs. Blossom.

"You look very charming in each of them, dearest. Personally I myself should purchase the one which is the most comfortable."

Lanthia considered this to be good advice, so she was extravagant enough to buy three of the prettiest hats on offer and was still considering another one.

What were really exciting were the evening gowns, which they had left until the afternoon.

Her mother had given her the name of a particular shop and said that was where she always went herself. The manageress remembered her and was exceedingly anxious to please Lanthia.

"I remember her Ladyship telling me that you were

to make your debut last year, miss," she minced. "We had some very lovely gowns which I know would have suited you, but I understand you are in mourning."

"For my dear grandfather," Lanthia answered her. "So now you must find me even prettier gowns than those I missed last year!"

The manageress laughed.

Every gown she deemed suitable was now shown to Lanthia and again she found it difficult to decide which she liked the best.

Finally she chose one gown which she thought was the most outstanding and she was promised faithfully that it would be ready for fitting the following day.

"It will take us quite a bit of time to alter it," said the manageress, "but I assure you there will be no one else in any ballroom wearing a more gorgeous gown!"

There were many more dresses that Lanthia wanted to see, but she soon realised Mrs. Blossom was becoming very tired.

After all they had been working, if that was the right word, since first thing in the morning and now it was getting on for teatime.

"I think we should leave the rest of our shopping until tomorrow," said Lanthia reluctantly and saw the relief on Mrs. Blossom's face.

When they hailed a Hackney Carriage and started back towards *The Langham*, Mrs. Blossom confessed to a headache.

"I am not used to London," she grumbled, "and I suppose that is why I did not sleep very well last night."

"You must lie down at once," suggested Lanthia, "and if you still feel tired, have dinner in bed."

"You cannot go into the dining room alone," Mrs.

Blossom answered quickly.

"No, of course not. I will either have dinner with you or in the sitting room. Don't worry at all. We have done a good day's work and there are not so many things we shall require tomorrow."

She thought Mrs. Blossom looked relieved again.

When they arrived at the hotel, Lanthia hurried her into the lift up to the second floor, but even so it was quite a long walk to their rooms.

Lanthia promised she would order some tea.

"You must get into bed and rest while you have the chance and thank you for being so kind and helpful to me."

"I have enjoyed every moment of it," Mrs. Blossom replied. "It is just this stupid head of mine which will ache when I do not want it to."

"I expect that means you are using your brain too much," smiled Lanthia.

At the same time she thought that Mrs. Blossom did indeed look very tired.

She took her into her bedroom first, made sure she was comfortable and then going back to her own room, she put the key into the lock of the sitting room door.

As she turned it she was suddenly aware that there was a man close behind her.

*

The Marquis of Rakecliffe drove down Piccadilly in his smart chaise which he had recently purchased.

It was drawn by two perfectly matched stallions of which he was particularly proud.

He would have been blind or very stupid if he had not noticed that every pedestrian walking along the pavement stared at him as he passed.

Where the men were concerned there was a look of admiration and envy in their eyes. It was just not only his horses, but the Marquis himself looked outstanding.

Broad-shouldered and extremely handsome he wore his hat at an angle which enhanced his appearance and also made his nickname seem appropriate.

He had been christened Victor James, but from the time he had been at Eton everyone had called him simply 'Rake'.

And that was undoubtedly what he had become.

Every woman he met pursued him relentlessly and he would have been inhuman if he had not accepted their many favours.

However, there was a serious side to his nature.

Most people were unaware that he had a very astute brain and was a brilliant organiser and it was the Prime Minister, Benjamin Disraeli, who was certainly the first to appreciate it.

The Marquis had always been a keen traveller and an explorer of different countries and the Prime Minister had been clever enough to realise how useful he could be.

Whenever he learned that the Marquis was going abroad, he would send for him and ask him to undertake a mission which he considered of great national importance.

"Not another mission?" the Marquis had groaned when he had found himself alone with the Prime Minister at number 10 Downing Street.

"There is just a small task you can undertake for me this time, Rake," said the Prime Minister. "And you know as well as I do that it is not something I can request from anyone else and expect the same result!"

The Marquis recognised that this was indeed true.

Because of his rank, great wealth and importance in

the Social world, he could enter places that were barred to other people. He could have conversations with those who would speak to no one else.

He had therefore been of immense service to the Prime Minister on various occasions.

Although he had always protested at what he was asked to do, he actually enjoyed the excitement and often the danger of it.

At that moment, however, he was not thinking of anything particularly serious.

He was cheerfully contemplating the extraordinary and unusual beauty of the woman he was about to visit.

He was well aware, when he saw the Contessa de Vallecas at a ball last night, that she had been manoeuvring for some time to arouse his interest in her.

It was not that difficult as she was an exceptionally beautiful woman and she oozed a seductive manner which several men before the Marquis had found irresistible.

The problem was that the Conté, her husband, was exceedingly and fanatically jealous of her. He had, it was whispered, killed two men in duels and maimed a number of others.

The Marquis was not quite certain that he believed these stories. However there was no point in running into danger or causing an unnecessary scandal.

He was very proud of his antecedents and had no wish to upset his family, who he recognised were watching him nervously.

The only means they could think of to prevent him from pursuing and being pursued by beautiful women was that he should be married to a socially acceptable lady as soon as possible.

Because they were so persistent and made such a

fuss about him, he had announced firmly to them that he had no intention of marrying at all.

"I like being a bachelor," he told them, "and wish to remain one."

As far as he was concerned, if he died without an heir, there were quite a number of his relatives who could easily take his place at the head of the family.

Of course his decision to remain single was known to a far wider public than just his close family.

Everything he did was always spectacular and he would have been inhuman if he had not, to a certain extent, found such attention to be amusing.

He had only to appear at any race meeting for the crowd to shout,

"Rake! Rake! Rake!"

"Good luck and God bless you!"

"May your horse win!"

They would shout a thousand more such greetings at him until he was out of sight.

His horses almost invariably won, which made him extremely popular, except with the bookmakers.

His carriages, like the colours worn by his jockeys, were painted bright yellow and this distinction only added to the glamour surrounding him.

Considering his fine looks combined with what was described as 'an irresistible charm,' it was not surprising that women had only to look at him to tell themselves that they were in love.

As the Marquis had no wish to be married, he was wise enough to keep away from *debutantes* and he avoided like the plague the many plots which were set for unwary bachelors by ambitious Society mothers.

It had given him a sharp warning when a friend of his, Lord Worcester, was forced into marriage with a girl he had merely talked to alone in the garden of a country house while he was enjoying a surreptitious cigarette that was not permitted inside.

The girl's mother had said that her reputation was ruined because she had been found alone with him and un-chaperoned.

She had persuaded the Prince of Wales to tell Lord Worcester he must behave like a gentleman and marry her daughter.

This story spread very quickly around all the Clubs in St. James's and it was a red warning to all bachelors who had no wish to be dragged to the altar.

The Marquis had listened to the jokes made at poor Worcester's expense and his fate had merely strengthened his resolve never to be married and to continue to 'play the field'.

However he was wise enough to be wary of jealous husbands.

The Prince of Wales had set a new fashion when he found himself infatuated with a lady who had become his mistress and was at the same time accepted by Society.

Attitudes had certainly changed considerably and it was Lillie Langtry, with her exquisitely beautiful face and lovely eyes, who was responsible for this Social revolution.

The Prince of Wales escorted Lillie everywhere and he insisted that she should be invited to every house where he stayed and every party he attended.

It was just impossible for the Social world to refuse him.

Only a number of the older Dowagers were deeply shocked at what they considered to be a new immorality that would never have been accepted even ten years ago.

In their day gentlemen indeed kept their mistresses, but such a practice was spoken of with bated breath behind closed doors.

There was no question of the mistress being seen with her protector outside the house he provided for her in Chelsea or in St. John's Wood, but there were, of course, a selection of restaurants and nightclubs where he could take her without meeting anyone from his own background.

But the Prince of Wales himself had now opened the floodgates to something new and very different and he was quickly copied by his friends and those who liked to think they were in his 'Marlborough House set'.

This new morality meant that a number of husbands were expected to close their eyes to the way their wives were misbehaving.

Some went shooting and fishing in other parts of the country, while the majority skulked in their Clubs at the times they were not expected to be at home.

They merely refused to believe anything untoward was happening.

At teatime a husband was not expected to intrude into his wife's boudoir and he was only welcomed home when it was time to change for dinner.

The Marquis, of course, took full advantage of this state of affairs, but all the same there were exceptions to the rule.

The Marquis was told by a dozen of his friends to steer clear of the Contessa de Vallecas.

He recognised that this was excellent advice, but the Contessa certainly had very different intentions. Inez, which was her name, made that very clear to him.

From the moment the Marquis had first touched her hand he sensed that she wished to see more of him.

They met at several fashionable dinner parties and had one dance at an important ball.

The Marquis had been aware when he put his arm round her thin sinuous body that she desired to grow closer to him and she told him without words that he would find it most enjoyable.

He had to admit that her beauty stood out.

Her extremely dark hair with blue lights in it and her green eyes made most English women look insipid.

Her skin was white as marble.

Every word she spoke and every movement of her hands and body were provocative.

She was undoubtedly a major challenge and that was something the Marquis had always found so hard to resist.

Last night at Marlborough House he had known as he looked at her across the dining room table that she was sending him a message with her eyes.

There was dancing after dinner and he deliberately waited until he had danced with Princess Alexandra and one or two other beautiful ladies before he approached the Contessa.

By that time it was getting late and she told him in a low voice that her husband wished to leave.

"Tomorrow he has to attend an appointment outside London," she whispered, "and I thought perhaps, my Lord, that you would like to take tea with me at four o'clock. We are staying at *The Langham*."

"I never drink tea," replied the Marquis.

"Nor do I," the Contessa answered coquettishly.

She looked up at him laughing and then she said,

"I will offer you something *very* different."

"Something new, Contessa? I think that is rather unlikely."

Her green eyes seemed to almost gleam at him as a tigress's might have done.

Then she replied,

"I promise you will find something very different in room 200!"

He felt it was impossible to refuse this fascinating invitation and he nodded,

"Very well, *Excelentisima Señora*, I will be there."

He deliberately used the Spanish manner in which she was usually addressed by her inferiors and because she understood that he was teasing her, she merely laughed.

"Your Lordship is too kind and it would be such a pity for you to be disappointed."

"A great pity," agreed the Marquis.

He turned away from her just as the Conté, who had been talking to the Prince of Wales, came to her side.

He was a somewhat dark man, a little taller than most Spaniards and good-looking in his own way, but he had a kind of ferociousness about him which made people feel he was more like a savage animal.

One which could easily get out of control.

The Marquis thought the suspicious way he looked at him was almost insulting.

He merely bowed formally to the Contessa, gave her husband a brief nod and walked away.

*

It was on the following morning that the Marquis remembered that he had promised to visit the Contessa.

He thought that if he was sensible it was something he should not do, but equally she had challenged him and it was against his nature not to accept a challenge.

The Marquis was naturally astute enough to check

that as she had said, the Conté was actually going to the country.

He had a friend who he knew was trying to interest the Conté in a new machinery development that could be a great advantage to the Spaniards.

He had no wish to ignite gossip about himself and the Contessa, so he casually dropped in to see his friend before luncheon and the Marquis found that the Conté had already left London.

The Marquis had learned what he wanted to know and so he left a message and drove to where he was having luncheon, which was with an extremely attractive lady who had held his attention for nearly three months.

He had, however, admitted to himself several nights ago that, as far as he was concerned, their *affaire-de-coeur* had come to an end.

As usual he had become bored, but the object of his affection was even more eager to keep him at her side than she had been in the first place.

The breaking off period was always unpleasant, but because she had arranged this luncheon party especially for him, the Marquis had felt obliged to attend it as it would have been too unkind not to do so.

The beauty in question was fair, blue-eyed and very English and undoubtedly most attractive.

Yet all through luncheon, at which there were six of his more intimate friends, the Marquis kept visualising the dark hair of the Contessa.

The glint of fire in her green eyes was completely unforgettable.

Because the party was so amusing, the conversation witty and the food and drink excellent, no one wished to leave.

Only the Marquis became aware after a while that his hostess was longing to be rid of her other guests, as she wanted to be alone with him.

It was the one confrontation he wished to avoid, but no one made a move to leave.

It was half past three when he rose to his feet and there was a little cry of resentment when he did so.

"You are not leaving us so soon, Rake?" asked the beauty he had found so attractive three months ago.

"I am afraid I have to go," he replied. "I do have an appointment at precisely four o'clock this afternoon and I must not be late."

She now looked at him reproachfully and with what he knew was also a look of despair.

He was very conscious that she was counting on this moment for them to be alone and she was obviously thinking that she could make him as ardent in his pursuit of her as he had been last February.

"Forgive me," said the Marquis as he took her hand in his. "I am very grateful to you for all your kindness."

For a second her fingers clung to his.

She knew he was saying goodbye and she wanted to throw herself on her knees and beg him not to go.

Just for one second they looked into each other's eyes and then the Marquis moved away towards the door.

Outside, as he stepped into his chaise and picked up the reins, he knew he had escaped lightly. He was afraid of tears and recriminations and the inevitable question,

"What have I done to lose your love?"

He had heard those words so often.

Yet he had never intended to hurt any woman, let alone one who had given him her heart.

It was just that inevitably he found, after quite a short time, they bored him.

It was something he had fought against, something he told himself he was not feeling – yet he did.

He could never explain to himself why, when they had all seemed wildly attractive, desirable and passionately exciting, they could suddenly become so banal.

He knew before they spoke what they were going to say and that knowledge, he reasoned, was the real reason why they bored him.

It was impossible for him to pretend that he was not bored when he was.

Now as he drove his chaise away from the house he had visited so often, he realised that he would never go back and there was nothing he could do to make the parting less poignant than it had been.

Then as he turned his horses down Bond Street, he felt that inevitable sparkle of excitement coursing through his veins.

He was chasing something new, something thrilling that was entirely different.

It was a sensation he always felt at the beginning of an *affaire-de-coeur*, only to find far too quickly and before he himself was even ready for it, that the chase was over.

He had known last night that the few words he had spoken to the Contessa had ignited a little fire inside him.

She told him that there was something sensational for him to uncover with her, which would be different from anything he had known before.

He could not imagine what it could be, but there was always a chance it would be fantastic.

He was not certain what he was looking for or what he desired and yet he was drawn, as if by a magnet, to the temptress with green eyes who was waiting for him.

When he reached *The Langham*, he drew his horses up outside the front entrance and as he handed his reins over to the hotel groom, he ordered,

"Come back in an hour and a half."

"Very good, my Lord."

The Marquis stepped out of his chaise and walked up the steps into the marble hall with enormous palm trees in each corner.

Several guests were enjoying early tea and because he knew the way, he walked past them.

Instead of taking the lift he decided to walk up the stairs. He knew the hotel well and was a frequent visitor.

None of the servants in attendance bothered to ask him what he wanted or who he wished to visit.

He was, however, surprised that the Contessa was on the second floor.

He supposed the hotel was over full, because it was the beginning of the Season and a large number of visitors at this time of year came from overseas.

Room number 200 was easy to find halfway down a side corridor.

The Marquis was not in the least fazed to find the door of the sitting room was unlocked.

When he turned the handle the door opened and he entered to find the room was just a mass of flowers. The fragrance of them, together with an exotic French perfume, filled the air.

There was no one in the room, but the door was ajar at the far end, which he assumed led into the bedroom.

The Marquis put his hat down on the nearest chair and walked towards it.

He pushed the door open to find that the curtains had been drawn and there was only a dim light on one side of the large four-poster bed.

There were more flowers everywhere just as there had been in the sitting room and their fragrance even more overpowering.

Then, lying on the bed, he could just make out the shadowy outline of the Contessa.

She was naked with the exception of three rows of black pearls around her neck.

For a moment she did not move and as the Marquis stood staring at her, she threw her long white arms towards him.

He walked nearer to the bed.

Then, with his eyes twinkling and a slightly cynical smile on his lips, he remarked,

"I think, Inez, you are rather over-dressed!"

Bending down he undid the pearls around her neck.

*

It was over an hour later that the Marquis arranged his tie in front of the mirror.

"Must you, my marvellous lover, leave so soon?" the Contessa crooned at him in her soft seductive voice.

"We shall meet tonight," he replied. "As you well know the Duke of Sutherland is holding a large party here and I need to go home to change."

"When shall I be with you again?" she implored, turning from the mirror.

"That is now in the lap of the Gods."

The Marquis picked up his coat which was lying on the chair.

As he was fastening it, the bedroom door burst open and a woman rushed in.

"Señora, Señora," she cried, "the Señor himself is on his way upstairs!"

The Contessa gave a scream of horror.

The Marquis without speaking, now rushed into the sitting room, seized his hat and pulled open the door into the corridor.

Even as he passed through it he thought he saw a figure approaching from the far end of the corridor and he turned in the other direction.

He moved very quickly, but at the same time he was aware it would be impossible for the Conté not to notice him.

The corridor was a long one and the Marquis was wondering what he would do when he reached the end.

Then he realised it turned and just ahead of him at the first door he could see, there was a young woman about to enter her room.

He pushed her forward and closed the door quickly behind them both.

Then as she made a small sound of fear and turned to look at him nervously, he said,

"I am the Marquis of Rakecliffe and I desperately need your help. Please will you agree to anything I say? *It is a question of life or death.*"

As Lanthia stared at him in sheer astonishment, the door behind them opened.

CHAPTER THREE

The Conté burst headlong into the room and faced the Marquis who was standing beside Lanthia.

"I saw you coming out from my wife's room!" he roared. "How dare you go in there? You have insulted me and I demand – "

The Marquis realised that this Spaniard was about to challenge him to a duel!

It was not because he was frightened that he did not wish to face the Conté in combat, but because duelling had been strictly forbidden by Queen Victoria.

Duels did take place secretly in Green Park, but if it was discovered, the duellists were forced to go abroad into exile for a year or perhaps two.

And that was something the Marquis did not wish for under any circumstances.

Nor did he relish the scandal of being challenged by the Conté.

He recognised immediately that the drama of two aristocrats from different countries confronting each other in a duel would inevitably reach the newspapers.

He held up his hand and in a voice even louder and more aggressive than the Conté, he called,

"Stop! You are making a mistake!"

"I am not making a mistake and you are a liar!" the Conté snapped.

"I have been shopping with this lady," the Marquis asserted in a firm but quieter tone, "and I think it would be polite if I introduced you – "

He turned towards Lanthia, who was listening with eyes wide with horror.

She was holding under her arm one of the parcels she had brought with her from the dress shop and she had been given a letter which had been waiting for her at the reception desk.

As she had unlocked the door with her right hand she had held both the parcel and the letter in her left.

The Marquis could read the name on the letter and speaking deliberately slowly he intoned,

"Please allow me to present the Conté de Vallecas, who has clearly mistaken me for someone else and I would like you, Conté, to meet Miss Lanthia Grenville, who has paid me the great honour of graciously promising to be my wife!"

For a moment the Conté, who had been bursting to interrupt him, was stunned into silence.

"*Your wife!*" he repeated as if he could not believe what he had heard. "Has the elusive Marquis of Rakecliffe been captured at last? I do not believe it for a moment!"

"I can assure you," said the Marquis, "that I am the luckiest man in the world. But what I have just told you is a close secret and must not be revealed to anyone because we have not yet informed our relations."

"If you really expect me to believe all that," snarled the Conté, "you are very much mistaken. I demand, as I have every right to do, that you make reparation!"

Again the Marquis held up his hand.

"You forget yourself, Vallecas. You are now in the presence of a lady. If you really do wish to discuss your allegation, which as I have already said is completely and absolutely untrue, then we should do so when my fiancée is not present."

The Conté wavered.

He believed the Marquis was lying, but at the same time as an aristocrat he could not degrade himself by being too offensive to someone of his own standing.

"I will make you pay for this insult, Rakecliffe!" he growled.

Then he stormed out of the room and slammed the door behind him.

The Marquis drew a deep sigh of relief as he knew that he had been standing on the very edge of disaster and had saved himself by only a hair's breadth.

He turned towards Lanthia and speaking in his most charming voice, which most women found irresistible, he said,

"Please forgive me, I would not have subjected you to this unpleasant scene if, as I have already said, it was not a question of life or death."

"He – intended," Lanthia murmured anxiously, "to challenge you – to a duel?"

It was the first words she had spoken and her voice trembled.

"You are quite right," responded the Marquis, "that is just what he intended and he is notorious for his success in duels. In fact it is widely rumoured he has already killed two men."

Lanthia gave a cry of horror.

"Then I am very glad you are now safe from him. But just suppose he tells everyone we are engaged!"

"I think as a gentleman, albeit a Spanish one, he will stay silent, but it was the only way I could save myself from a most unpleasant duel. Moreover Her Majesty the Queen has very strictly forbidden duelling to take place."

Lanthia gave a sigh.

Then as if she suddenly became aware she was still carrying a parcel, she put it down on a side-table and laid the letter on top of it.

"I was fortunate in being able to read your name on the letter," admitted the Marquis. "I assume you really are Miss Lanthia Grenville."

Lanthia smiled.

"Yes, that is indeed my name and it was lucky the letter from my mother was waiting for me downstairs."

"I was just wondering what I should call you, for of course if the Conté had found the name I gave you was not true, it would have added to his suspicions which I regret to say are already rampant."

"So you *were* visiting his wife?"

"The Contessa, who is a charming lady, invited me to take tea with her. It is well known that her husband is frantically jealous and I would have been wiser to refuse."

"But do you think you are safe now?"

The Marquis was silent for a moment and then he answered,

"My old Nanny always used to teach me that one lie leads to another and I am afraid I am still in a desperate position unless you continue to help me."

Lanthia looked at him wide-eyed.

He now realised for the first time that she was very attractive. In fact she was extremely beautiful in her own way, just as the Contessa was beautiful in hers.

The Marquis walked to the window and stood for a moment looking down onto Portland Place.

There were many carriages moving on the road and it reminded him that his own horses were waiting.

He was, however, turning over in his mind what he should say to Lanthia, who had just taken off her gloves and was now removing her hat.

Just as she set it down, the sunshine streamed in through the window and turned her hair to gold.

'She is lovely, in fact more beautiful than any girl I have seen for a long time,' the Marquis told himself.

He turned towards her saying,

"The way you can help me, if you would be so kind as to continue to do so – and it is difficult for me to express my eternal gratitude – is to attend a dinner party with me here tonight."

"*A dinner party*?" repeated Lanthia.

"It is being given by a very close friend of mine, the Duke of Sutherland, and the Conté and the Contessa of Vallecas will be among the guests."

"You mean," said Lanthia slowly, "that the Conté will think it strange if you are there without me."

"He will not only think it very strange indeed," the Marquis replied, "but he will doubtless call me a liar again and challenge me to make reparation for what he considers to be an insult."

"Then what can you do?"

"It is actually, Miss Grenville, a matter of what *you* will do! I am asking you to take pity on me and attend this party, which I think you will find very enjoyable and allay the Conté's suspicions at least until tomorrow."

He was hoping as he spoke that the Contessa would have the intelligence to deny that he had been with her.

She had undoubtedly undertaken a number of love affairs when her husband was absent and she had thought that today she would be safe from discovery and so she could consequently deny all his accusations.

At the same time the Marquis thought that if he was indeed engaged, it would be highly unlikely that he would attend the Sutherland party without his fiancée.

Even if their engagement was a secret one it would still look suspicious to the Conté.

He was a very dangerous man and the Marquis now realised that he needed to contrive somehow or another to convince him that he was speaking the truth.

He could not imagine why he had been so foolish.

He had been unbelievably tempted by Inez to come to her bedroom and he should have refused if there was the slightest possibility of her husband returning earlier than expected.

'I was a complete fool', the Marquis told himself.

Equally he had always taken risks in his life and as one of his friends had remarked about him,

"There is no one quicker than Rake at getting into trouble and no one cleverer at getting out of it!"

Speaking again in a voice he knew was appealing, he pleaded,

"Please, Miss Grenville, save me. As I expect you know, it is always a mistake to upset or enrage our foreign visitors. Her Majesty is very anxious that we should be at peace with those of significance in Europe."

"I thought," commented Lanthia, "that he was a most sinister looking man and you must be careful that he does not hurt you as he obviously intends to do."

"The first thing I have to do is to convince him that I was not endangering his relationship with his wife. He will be looking for you this evening and will be extremely suspicious if you are not there! So I can only beg you to accompany me to the Duke's party."

"But surely the Duke will think it very strange?"

"I have known the Duke for a long time and he is a good friend of mine. If I ask a favour of him, he will not refuse me."

He felt that Lanthia was wavering and so he put out his hand.

"Please," he pleaded again, "do not throw me to the wolves. Or in this case a very savage Spaniard!"

Lanthia gave a laugh because she could not help it.

"I will come to the dinner party," she agreed, "but I only hope I will not do anything to make matters worse for you than they are already."

"On the contrary you will save me, Miss Grenville, and I can assure you that I shall be eternally grateful."

He glanced at the clock on the mantelpiece.

"I must return to my own house and change into my evening clothes. I will collect you from here just before eight o'clock. That is when we are asked to arrive and I imagine dinner will be at half-past eight.

"Please put on your very prettiest gown and I am certain that everyone when they see you will realise why I wanted you to be my wife."

"I think from what the Conté was saying that you have a reputation of preferring to be a bachelor."

The Marquis thought that was clever of her and he replied,

"You are absolutely right, Miss Grenville, or rather, may I call you, Lanthia? I must get used to calling you by your Christian name! I have a horror of marriage and I am determined to remain a bachelor until I am in my dotage!"

Lanthia giggled.

"I can now understand why the Conté became so incredulous when you introduced him to your fiancée!"

"I believe I sounded reasonably convincing, but I will have to be even more convincing this evening. And I am totally banking on his behaving decently and keeping our engagement a secret."

Lanthia gave a little cry.

"What shall we do if he tells everyone?"

"I don't think he will, Lanthia, as it would be too much of a cad's trick and the Conté, unpleasant though he is, comes from one of the oldest families in Spain. No one can say he is not an aristocrat!"

"Then our pretend engagement," added Lanthia, as if she was working it out for herself, "need not be for very long."

"Shall we say for just as long as you stay here at *The Langham*?" suggested the Marquis.

"I expect to leave here in two or at the outside three days."

"Then it will not require a great deal of acting and let me thank you for being so kind and understanding and very much braver and more sensible than any other woman would ever have been."

He thought as he spoke he was very lucky that she had not simply denied what he had invented on the spur of the moment. She might easily have told both him and the Conté to leave her sitting room at once.

Because he really was extremely grateful, he raised her hand to his lips.

"You have been so wonderful already," he told her, "and I am asking you to be even more wonderful again tonight. I will try not to be more of a nuisance than I can help."

50

"I cannot believe this is really happening," Lanthia sighed.

He knew from the way she spoke that it really did seem to her like something out of a book or a scene from a play.

"I am so very fortunate, Lanthia, to have found you. Now I must hurry as I need to write a note to the Duke and leave it on the way to my house."

He picked up his hat and walked towards the door.

"Until ten minutes to eight," he bowed, "and try to look even more beautiful than you do at the moment."

It was a compliment he would have made to any of the beauties with whom he was usually associated.

He saw Lanthia's eyes widen in surprise and then a faint colour came into her cheeks.

'She is very young,' he told himself as he walked down the stairs. 'At the same time few young girls would have shown such self-control or would have behaved so well. I do believe we have really got the Conté guessing, even if he is not yet entirely convinced.'

He was pondering that he had contrived so many harrowing escapes in his life, but this easily was one of the nearest.

In the writing room on the ground floor he wrote a quick note to the Duke of Sutherland.

He told him that a young lady to whom he owed a great debt of gratitude had arrived in London unexpectedly and he would be eternally grateful if he might bring her to the party tonight.

"*I will explain more about it,*" he ended, "*the next time we are alone and I know the story will amuse you.*

Please grant me this favour.

Yours,

Rake."

He had known the Duke for many years and every autumn he would stay at Dunrobin Castle in Sutherland to shoot grouse. The Duke was very fond of him.

The Duke and his wife Anne were almost totally estranged from each other. He had become infatuated with various pretty women when the Duchess as Mistress of the Robes to the Queen joined the Court at Windsor Castle.

The Duke was frequently with the Prince of Wales as a member of the fast set to which His Royal Highness was openly attached.

Another member of the set was the very beautiful German born Duchess of Manchester who, it was said, had a number of distinguished lovers.

The Duke of Sutherland owned four stately homes, a number of smaller houses and a million and a half acres of land.

It was just by chance that tonight he was holding his party at *The Langham*, as he was having several rooms redecorated at his London mansion, Stafford House, and the contractors had overrun their time.

Stafford House was well known as one of the most impressive and attractive houses in London.

It was where Queen Victoria had said to the Duke's mother, Harriet, Duchess of Sutherland,

"I come from my house to your Palace!"

The Marquis recognised that it was unusual for the Duke to entertain anywhere other than under his own roof, but an American who he had stayed with in New York had arrived in London unexpectedly.

It was impossible therefore to give a party for him at Stafford House with so many workmen still in the best reception rooms

Also, the Marquis had learned, he was only staying

two days in London and the Duke had therefore arranged a large dinner party for over fifty of his guests to be held at *The Langham*.

The Marquis's chaise was waiting for him outside and he drove as fast as possible to Stafford House, where the groom handed in his note.

Without waiting for an answer he drove on to his house in Park Lane and by the time he arrived it was after seven o'clock.

It was with a sense of relief that, as no one was staying with him, the Marquis could go straight up to his bedroom and change for dinner and his valet already had his bath arranged for him in front of the fireplace.

When he had bathed and was dressing, he reflected that what had occurred this afternoon was something that had never happened to him before.

He could not comprehend why the idea of saying he was engaged to Lanthia Grenville had suddenly sprung into his mind.

He could have invented some other explanation as to why he was in a room alone with a pretty woman.

He had hardly been given a chance to look at her before the Conté burst in.

When he did he realised how young she was, but at the same time quite obviously a lady.

Even so he thought it might have been expected of him that he was in the company of a pretty girl for very different reasons than that he was engaged to her.

'I must have sensed instinctively,' he told himself, 'that she might have been shocked and horrified at such a suggestion, nor would she have looked the part!'

Thinking it over he was convinced that because she looked so young and, to use an unusual word, *pure*, the

Conté had almost accepted the explanation that she was his fiancée.

And definitely not just a pretty woman who for the moment he had found desirable.

It was difficult for him to put it all into perspective and yet the Marquis knew that for the moment he had to fully convince the Conté tonight that Lanthia really meant something to him.

He would then, he hoped, desist from forcing him into a duel.

At exactly twenty minutes to eight he hurried down the stairs. The butler and two footmen were waiting in the hall to open the door and help him into his closed carriage. One of the footmen handed the Marquis his tall hat and another placed his evening cape round his shoulders.

Then the Marquis stepped into his carriage.

His coachman already had instructions as to where to take him.

*

At *The Langham* Lanthia was quite certain she was living in a dream.

Could it really be possible that these two men had burst into her sitting room?

Firstly the Marquis, who, she had to admit, was one of the most handsome men she could ever have imagined.

Secondly the Conté, who she instinctively realised was cruel, wicked and a man she would not trust.

He was dangerous. There was no doubt about that.

She was frightened that he would have his revenge somehow on the Marquis, however brave he might be.

She found it very hard to believe that she was really going to attend the very grand dinner party that was to take place here in the hotel this very evening.

She went in to see Mrs. Blossom and found that she was already in bed.

"Are you feeling any better?" Lanthia asked her.

"I shall be all right, dear child. It is just my head, but I am sure that after a good night's sleep I shall be myself again."

Lanthia was going to tell her about her invitation to the Duke's dinner party at the hotel, but then she thought it would be a mistake.

"What about your dinner?" she enquired instead.

"I want nothing when I am like this, my dear. All I want is to sleep and I confess that I am going to take a little laudanum. Only a little so that I shall sleep soundly."

"Then I hope nothing will disturb you,"

Lanthia bent down and kissed her.

"Thank you for being so kind to me today and I am sure the gowns we bought will be a great success."

"I am certain you will look very pretty in them all."

Mrs. Blossom closed her eyes and Lanthia tiptoed from the room.

Back in her sitting room she knew she had to hurry.

It was a blessing that she had brought with her the pretty gown her mother had given her last year for her birthday.

She had only worn it just a few times, but she still thought, even after viewing all those glamorous models today in the shops, that it was very attractive.

The gown became her as it was soft and white and it seemed to envelop her as if she was an angel floating on clouds in the sky.

She had not intended to bring it to London with her, but her mother had said,

"As it fits you so well, dearest, I should take it with you so that you can compare it with the gowns you buy. If you remember, we took a long time getting it made exactly as we wanted it to be."

Lanthia knew this to be true and it crossed her mind as she dressed that the Marquis might otherwise have been disappointed.

The gowns she usually wore when she was dining alone with her father and mother and the one she had worn last night with Mrs. Blossom were much simpler.

She put up her hair in the way her mother arranged it for parties.

When she was finally ready she looked at herself in the mirror. She was looking for faults, but could not find any.

In fact she thought that she looked smart enough to go to any party given by a Duke.

'I do hope I do not make any mistakes,' she said to herself. 'Equally it will all be very exciting and something to tell Mama about when I go home.'

It might have seemed rather shocking if it had been necessary to drive on to somewhere else with the Marquis without a chaperone and she knew her mother would have disapproved.

Now she would only have to walk downstairs with the Marquis and no one could say there was anything at all wrong in that.

She wondered vaguely what excuse he would give the Duke for bringing her to his party, but it did not seem to matter too much.

In fact because everything was happening to her in such a strange way, nothing seemed in any way real.

It was just like one of the stories she told herself as she rode through the woods.

At precisely a quarter to eight the Marquis knocked on the door of the sitting room and Lanthia opened it.

She had expected him to look very smart, but in his evening clothes he was overwhelming.

He saw at a glance that Lanthia was exactly as he wanted her to be.

It had struck him as just his good luck to discover anyone so exquisite and so perfect for the part he wanted her to play.

In fact he could not imagine there was a woman in the whole of the City of London who could look so lovely and so perfectly dressed for the occasion.

"I very much hope I will not do anything wrong tonight or make the Conté suspicious," said Lanthia, as he did not speak.

"I think anything you say or do will be completely and absolutely right," replied the Marquis eventually. "I am thinking of all the compliments you will receive tonight and it is fortunate that unlike the Conté I will not challenge everyone to a duel who makes them!"

Lanthia laughed as he had meant her to do.

"I am sure that will not happen, but tell me quickly about our host tonight. I have been trying to think if I have ever heard anything about him."

"I expect you have," replied the Marquis, "because he is, in his own way, quite famous. He is married, but he and the Duchess more or less live their own lives."

Lanthia was listening and he continued,

"The Duchess is very religious and when in London she attends the Church of Scotland with her own piper in full ceremonial dress sitting beside her!"

Lanthia gave a little laugh and then wondered if she

had been rude.

"When she is at home in Stafford House, she reads novels lying on a sofa under a red satin eiderdown. She is surrounded by many mynah birds and parrots who perch on everything including the head of her old retriever!"

Lanthia chuckled again.

"What does the Duke do about it?" she asked.

The Marquis's eyes twinkled.

"Come and see for yourself," he said mysteriously and escorted her through the door.

They walked down the corridor with the Marquis praying that the two Spaniards would not come out of their room as they passed their door.

He thought it might make things more difficult than they were already if they were forced to go down in the lift together.

Downstairs the Duke's guests were already arriving and pouring in through the hall.

The Marquis had already attended several formal dinner parties at *The Langham* and he reckoned that the Duke would have taken the whole of the large dining room, which was known as the *salle à manger*.

To reach it they were required to pass through a small courtyard with a fountain playing in the middle of it.

Lanthia had never seen this fountain before and she wanted to stop and admire it, thinking just how fascinating it was.

The water caught the lights as it streamed towards the sky and turned into tiny rainbows.

The Marquis however moved her on.

They walked up some steps to the entrance to the *salle à manger* where the Duke was receiving his guests.

He held out his hand to the Marquis.

"I am delighted to see you, Rake, and of course to meet your friend you wanted to bring with you."

"May I introduce her?" asked the Marquis. "Miss Lanthia Grenville – the Duke of Sutherland."

"I am so delighted to welcome you, Miss Grenville, and I do hope you will enjoy yourself tonight," the Duke greeted her.

"It is very kind of you to invite me," she replied.

The Duke was looking at the Marquis.

"The hatching is going well," he said, "and we shall have plenty of grouse for you at Dunrobin in the autumn."

"I am much looking forward to the beginning of the shooting Season."

They moved on because there were so many other guests behind them.

The Marquis located the seating plan and noted that the party was arranged in tables of ten, except for the one in the centre at which twenty people were seated.

As he expected it was where he was placed.

Lanthia's name had clearly been written in at the last moment and was seated on his left.

He realised that he must have caused a great deal of trouble in upsetting the seating plan at the last moment and he could only be very grateful to the Duke for acceding to his request.

He was most relieved to find that the Conté and the Contessa were seated at another table.

It was then, as they were studying the seating plan, that Lanthia gave a little gasp and the Marquis noticed who she was pointing at, placed at the top of their table.

It was the Prince of Wales.

And beside him and this came as no surprise at all – Mrs. Lillie Langtry.

"You did not tell me," murmured Lanthia, "that the Prince of Wales would be present."

"I did not know either," admitted the Marquis, "and if you have never met him you will find him very charming and easy to talk to."

Lanthia did not answer and the Marquis realised with slight amusement that she did not look frightened or upset, only what he could only describe as enchanted.

'She is certainly most unusual for a young girl,' he thought.

There were many guests whom he knew and who called out his name.

It was the gentlemen who said,

"Hello, Rake, and what are you up to now?" or words to that effect.

The ladies looked at him in a way that seemed a little familiar, which informed him all too clearly what they wanted but could not put into words.

There were several waiters circulating and offering everyone a glass of champagne.

Lanthia took a glass and sipped it carefully.

At home her parents opened a bottle of champagne only on very special occasions and she knew it would be a mistake to drink too much.

It might make her say something she might regret later.

The Prince of Wales and Lillie Langtry were almost the last of the guests to arrive.

As he entered the *salle à manger*, the ladies nearest to them sank into deep curtsies as the gentlemen bowed.

Lanthia and the Marquis were standing at the other

end of the room and she asked him in a whisper,

"Who is that lady with the Prince of Wales? She does not look like Princess Alexandra."

"That is Mrs. Langtry. Surely you must have heard of '*the Jersey Lily*', who has taken London by storm."

"Yes, I have indeed heard about her and how she came to London with only one black dress."

The Marquis laughed.

"Everyone remembers that part of the story. Now she boasts a great number of gorgeous gowns and each one is as beautiful as she is herself!"

Lanthia was looking at her intently.

"She is extremely beautiful and even more beautiful than I expected her to be."

The Marquis was smiling to himself and wondering what more he could tell her about Lillie Langtry.

He was quite certain that as Lanthia was so young and unsophisticated she would have no idea that she had been the Prince of Wales's mistress for a long time.

He also knew Lillie Langtry quite intimately and it would be rather difficult to explain to someone as young as Lanthia how much she had changed Social attitudes since she came to London from Jersey.

It was Lord Ranelagh, whom she had met on a few occasions in Jersey where he owned a house, who had first introduced her to the Social world.

Lillie was the daughter of a clergyman, the Dean of Jersey and she was twenty-one and had been married for three years when she had persuaded her husband Edward Langtry to take her to London.

From the moment she first appeared in Society she caused a sensation, which was to have a more far-reaching result than anyone ever anticipated.

As soon as her intimate friendship with the Prince of Wales became common knowledge, large crowds came to look at her wherever she went.

Her photograph was on sale in many shops and if she went for a walk people ran after her. They would stare at her and even raise her sunshade to see her more closely.

The Prince of Wales had first encountered her when Princess Alexandra had been on an official visit to Greece.

The Marquis remembered how the Prince had taken no trouble to disguise his infatuation for Lillie Langtry.

The Marquis had smiled when he learned that the Prince had taken Lillie to Paris.

Gossips said he had kissed her on the dance floor at Maxim's!

What was even more amazing was that the Prince had arranged for Lillie and her husband to be presented to the Queen.

This completely astonished the Social world.

They had always been very strict in their behaviour towards what was called a 'fallen woman'. However they could not deny that the Prince of Wales and Mrs. Langtry were accepted by practically every fashionable hostess in London.

It was inevitable that the Marquis should become interested in Lillie Langtry.

He had been warned, before the Prince became her lover, that she had developed a special way of seducing a man who was a little nervous of succumbing to her charms.

She would just wait until they were alone and then, having hypnotised him with her huge blue eyes, she gave the appearance of fainting.

He would immediately support her on the sofa and she would be beautiful, helpless and limp in his arms.

He would do his best to revive her until her eyelids were flickering and it was clear that she was not actually going to die.

She had not had to pretend to faint to attract either the Prince of Wales or the Marquis, who now watched her moving gracefully through the room with the Prince.

He was thinking with a cynical smile that, however beautiful a woman might be, sooner or later she became a bore.

When they sat down at the table, Lanthia found she had an elderly Earl on her other side.

He was mainly interested in horses and although he paid her fulsome compliments, she found it easier to talk to him about the horses he would be running at Ascot than about herself.

The Marquis had a very alluring lady sitting on his other side and they were obviously old friends.

The first thing she wanted to know was who was Lanthia and why was she with him?

The Marquis told her casually that she was a good friend of his, who had just arrived from the West Country and as he was somewhat indebted to her father, he had contrived to bring her to the party.

It was only an attempt, he said, to pay back what he owed for a kindness in the past.

"She is *very* pretty," remarked his companion. "At the same time, dear Rake, you have surely not yet taken to cradle-snatching!"

"I can most definitely assure you," responded the Marquis nonchalantly, "I am not snatching anyone at the moment!"

"Then that makes me definitely even more worried about you," she retorted, "unless of course you are growing blind in your old age!"

The Marquis chortled.

"I can still see you and that, as you well know, is a sight I have always enjoyed."

He noticed a little flicker in her eyes and recognised that he must be most careful not to rekindle a fire that had already burned down.

He had learnt of old that this tactic was never a success and in fact could turn into a disaster.

When he turned again to talk to Lanthia, she said,

"I think this is a most glamorous and fascinating party and I still think I am in a dream."

"Then do not wake, because it would definitely be a mistake!" he smiled.

He pondered as he spoke, it was decidedly charming to see her to be so entranced with everything around her.

At the same time he considered she looked exactly as if she belonged.

Only he knew she had been pushed into the dinner party at the last moment to save him from a very dangerous situation.

He was not at that particular time aware of what would happen later on in the evening.

CHAPTER FOUR

Dinner was a rather long and drawn out affair.

Looking around the room the Marquis recognised that most of the guests were older than him and, of course, very much older than Lanthia.

Whilst they were eating an orchestra was playing quietly in the courtyard which made everything seem very romantic.

There was, however, obviously not going to be any dancing afterwards and when dinner was over, the guests moved about from one table to another talking to friends.

Some ambled into the courtyard to appreciate the orchestra, while the majority remained in the dining room and naturally clustered round the Prince of Wales and Mrs. Lillie Langtry.

The Marquis was wise enough to attempt to avoid the Prince of Wales, because they were old friends and he felt quite certain that the Prince would ask him who he was escorting. That would only complicate matters even more than they were already.

He thought anyway it would soon be time for His Royal Highness to leave the party.

The Marquis was talking to a friend at the other end of the room when the Prince's Equerry came up to him.

"His Royal Highness wishes to speak with you, my Lord," he announced, "and asks if you will bring with you the young lady you brought to the dinner party."

The Marquis stiffened.

He considered it most unlikely that the Duke had said anything to the Prince about his companion and there was only one person who could have done so, deliberately intending to make trouble.

There was nothing he could possibly do but to obey the summons.

He whispered quietly to Lanthia who was talking to an elderly lady,

"Please come with me."

She promptly excused herself to follow the Marquis and they walked over to where the Prince of Wales was holding court at the far end of the room.

As the Marquis approached the Prince turned away from the friends he was talking to and asked him,

"Are you neglecting me, Rake?"

"No, indeed not, sir," he replied. "But I felt you were very busy and I did not wish to interrupt you."

"I am always delighted to be interrupted by you, Rake!" said the Prince.

As he was talking to the Marquis he was looking directly at Lanthia.

She had curtsied when the Marquis had bowed to the Prince and was now standing a little way behind him.

He turned round to bring her forward.

"Please may I present, sir, Miss Lanthia Grenville."

The Prince put out his hand to her and she swept to the ground in another deep curtsy.

Then the Prince exclaimed,

"Enchanting! But I hear you have a secret you are keeping from me, Rake."

"You are quite right, sir, in saying it is a secret."

"Not to *me*," asserted the Prince of Wales firmly. "After all, as one of your oldest friends, Rake, I think that you might have told me what was happening before you told anyone else!"

There was a distinctly hurt note in his voice.

The Marquis realised only too well that the Prince suffered from severe frustration because his mother would not allow him to take any part in political affairs.

He therefore always wanted to be the first to know any secrets which concerned his friends and acquaintances.

The Marquis lowered his voice to speak directly into the Prince's ear.

"What you have heard, sir, only happened today. It is unfortunate that the person who spoke to you became prematurely aware of the story."

"Well, if it is indeed true," the Prince glowed, "I am absolutely delighted! It is just what we all hoped would happen sooner rather than later!"

Before the Marquis could say anything the Prince continued,

"I would like to take a closer look at the young lady who has succeeded where so many have failed!"

The Prince turned towards Lanthia and once again she curtsied to him.

"She is lovely, just perfectly lovely and of course I congratulate you, my dear Rake. Your taste has always been unerring and I am delighted that you are no longer the elusive Marquis!"

The Marquis laughed, but at the same time he was hoping that no one could overhear their conversation.

"You must tell me," the Prince addressed Lanthia, "where my friend the Marquis met you and why I have not seen you before."

"I live in the country, Your Royal Highness,"

The Marquis noticed and he felt it rather unusual that Lanthia was not the least shy at speaking to the Prince of Wales.

In similar circumstances so many would be almost paralysed with embarrassment, but she was just looking at him admiringly.

"Whereabouts in the country is your family home?" the Prince enquired.

"In Huntingdonshire, sir."

"A very attractive County. As I was saying to your Lord Lieutenant only a few weeks ago – I expect you know him?"

"Yes, indeed, sir. He is a friend of my parents and we are all attending the ball he is giving next month for Her Majesty the Empress of Austria."

"That is certainly something to greatly look forward to. As I shall doubtless be a guest on that occasion, I shall look forward to seeing you again."

Lanthia smiled at him.

"It will be most exciting for me to meet you again, Your Royal Highness."

The Prince was now looking closely at her and the Marquis was only too well aware that he was thinking how pretty she was.

Then the Prince continued,

"I have another idea. The Princess is returning late tonight, and I know, Rake, that she will want to meet your fiancée. Bring her to luncheon tomorrow and then you can tell me more about this secret of yours which is apparently only known to the Conté de Vallecas!"

There was nothing the Marquis could say, but that it would be a great honour and both he and Lanthia would be only too delighted to accept his invitation to luncheon at Marlborough House.

There were several other guests anxious to speak to the Prince of Wales, so they moved away.

As already a number of guests had left and others were saying their goodbyes to the Duke, the Marquis said to Lanthia in a low voice,

"I think we had better go, it is getting rather late."

Actually he was thinking that the sooner they were both out of sight the better.

If the Conté was walking round informing everyone they were engaged it would make life extremely difficult.

He would have to admit later it had just been a false alarm and he was not intending to break his vow to remain a bachelor.

He thought Lanthia looked round wistfully, but she did not say anything.

He so admired her self-control in keeping silent as any other woman would have pleaded with him to stay at the party longer.

Just as he had thought any other woman so young and apparently knowing so little of London Society would have been nervous at being presented to the Prince.

Lanthia had behaved quite naturally and correctly.

For the first time since they had met in such strange circumstances, the Marquis wondered who her father and mother were.

The Duke was now saying goodbye to his friends at the opening into the courtyard.

The Marquis was most effusive to him.

"Thank you a thousand times for such a delightful evening and for allowing me to bring Lanthia Grenville with me."

The Duke's eyes twinkled.

"She has embellished my party, Rake."

Lanthia thanked him as well and they walked into the courtyard.

Now that they were not in a hurry, Lanthia ran to the fountain. She stood looking up at the water as it swept up towards the sky making thousands of rainbows.

Watching her the Marquis felt she looked so lovely that any artist would wish to paint her.

Then glancing back he could see the Conté and the Contessa saying farewell to their host.

Taking Lanthia by the arm he hurried her out of the courtyard and up the steps into the other side of the hotel. They reached the lift and were taken to the second floor.

When the lift stopped, the Marquis walked quickly, still without speaking, towards Lanthia's room.

She kept her key in the pretty bag she carried which matched her dress and when she drew it out, the Marquis took it from her and opened the door.

Then as she entered he followed behind her.

She looked at him as if she was somewhat surprised that he should do so.

"I noticed the Spaniards were saying goodbye just after us," he explained, "and as I have no wish to speak to the Conté, I hope you will allow me to stay here for a short while until they are safely in their own suite and behind closed doors."

"Yes, of course," agreed Lanthia. "I saw him after dinner and I thought he was looking at you in a horribly revengeful way."

"He was thinking how he could make life difficult for me, which was why he told the Prince of Wales our secret."

"I just knew that was what he had done!" exclaimed

Lanthia, "and I think it is most dishonourable of him. But then he is a nasty sinister man!"

"I agree with you, Lanthia, and that is why I would like to wait a little time before I leave here."

He sank down in one of the armchairs in the sitting room and Lanthia said,

"I am afraid I have nothing to offer you. Of course, if Papa was here, he would ask you if you would like a 'night-cap'."

"Which would be very polite, but actually I want nothing, except I was thinking as we came away from the party that I have never asked you about your parents. In fact I did not even know you lived in Huntingdonshire."

"The reason why I am in London," she explained, "is that I have to buy a new gown for the ball that the Lord Lieutenant is giving for the Empress of Austria."

"To which you are going, and the Empress or no Empress, you will undoubtedly be the most beautiful lady present!"

Lanthia laughed.

"I don't believe it for a moment, but it is very kind of you to say so."

Then she asked in a very different tone of voice,

"What can we do about tomorrow? I know you do not want to take me to Marlborough House."

"It is something we shall have to do, Lanthia. I am turning over in my mind whether I shall tell the Prince the truth or allow him to think we are engaged until we decide we are not suited to each other."

"Which is the easiest for you?"

"I really do not know," the Marquis answered her. "You see, we will not be the only guests at Marlborough House and I am afraid that the Prince, who can be most talkative, will want to tell them all our secret. In fact, if he is telling people that you have managed to ensnare me and the Conté is doing the same, we might as well announce our engagement in *The Times* right away!"

He spoke bitterly with a touch of anger in his voice.

Then he saw that Lanthia, who was perched on the arm of a chair, was looking upset.

"I am very sorry," she said. "Perhaps it would be better if I just returned to the country immediately and then they would have nothing to gossip about."

"I think such a move would give them a great deal to discuss. I am beginning to fear that this masquerade, in which you have been forced to take part, will harm us as much as the Conté intends it to do."

"Then what can we do?" asked Lanthia. "Perhaps Papa and Mama will be very angry that I took part in it."

"But you were kind enough to save my life. Thus we have to be very clever and somehow extract ourselves from this dreadful mess, which is of course a deadly game which the Conté is playing to the full."

Lanthia sat back in the chair and clasped her hands in her lap.

"I am sure you will think of something. If only Mr. Richard Burton was staying in the hotel, I am sure he could help us. He managed to extract himself from very many dangerous situations when just a casual word would have brought about his death."

The Marquis looked at her in surprise.

"Do you know Richard Burton?" he enquired.

"Oh, I wish I did! He was staying in this hotel only a few months ago and it would have been so wonderful to have seen him."

The Marquis was astonished.

There was a note of admiration in her voice which he was accustomed to hear only when a lady was talking about himself.

"Why are you so impressed with Burton?" he now asked. "I have met him once or twice and naturally I much admire him and his many achievements."

"You have met him?" enthused Lanthia excitedly. "Oh, how lucky you are! I have read and re-read his books and, as I have just said, I am sure he would think of a way out of this difficult situation."

"Burton is certainly a past-master at disguise and of course a great explorer, which is why we had something in common when we met."

Lanthia looked at him with what he thought was an incredulous expression.

"Are you saying that you are an explorer too?"

"I have certainly travelled a great deal," replied the Marquis. "I have not been to Mecca like Richard Burton, but I have explored many other parts of the unknown world which I must say I found totally fascinating."

Lanthia sat forward in her chair.

"Oh, I do hope you will tell me about it," she cried. "Papa has told me all about his travels, and once when I was young he and Mama took me with them. I always hoped that when I had finished my education they would take me again."

She gave a little sigh before she added,

"Now I think they are too old, so I will just have to travel and explore the world in my mind. Although I find it all very thrilling, it is not quite the same as if I was really climbing a mountain or riding a camel across the desert!"

"You do astonish me, Lanthia, I have never yet met a woman of your age who wanted to do either of those things!"

"Those and so many more. I long to look at the Sphinx and discover its many secrets and I want more than anything else to visit Greece and visit the shining cliffs of Delphi."

Now there was a rapt note in her voice which made the Marquis stare at her.

He knew she was speaking with all sincerity and it astonished him that any woman should feel so elated and so excited just by the idea of exploring.

It was like what he felt himself.

He had always travelled alone and he realised only too well that, if a woman was with him, she would be only talking about love.

Or else complaining that he was not making her as comfortable as she wished to be.

"You say your father has travelled extensively," he said. "Rather late in our acquaintance, I do admit, but I should ask you now who your father is."

"You may well have read one of Papa's books on travel. They are just signed Philip Grenville, because three of his best volumes were published before he came into the Baronetcy."

The Marquis started.

"Of course I know your father's books, but it never struck me at all that the name was the same as yours. I have four, if not more of his books, in my library."

"Well if you have read them, you will understand why I have always wanted to travel as he has and I hoped that when I was old enough he would take me on some wonderful expeditions, perhaps to discover the source of the Nile or journey into Tibet which is where he has always wanted to explore."

"And where I have been – " replied the Marquis.

Lanthia gave a cry.

"You have actually been there! Tell me all about it. Tell me what you actually felt. I have read a dozen books on Tibet, but I have never met anyone who has actually been there!"

The Marquis smiled.

"Then I will certainly relate to you everything I can remember, but I think now, as it is getting late and I am quite sure our enemies are locked into their own rooms, I should leave you."

He rose slowly to his feet and added as if it was just an afterthought,

"Surely you are not staying here alone."

"No, of course not. I have a dear friend of Mama's, a charming Mrs. Blossom, who is the only daughter of the Bishop of Bristol and who is my chaperone."

She hoped that the Marquis was impressed as she continued,

"She contracted a headache this afternoon and as she wanted to go to sleep and not be disturbed, I did not tell her I was dining downstairs with you."

"I think that was most wise of you and we shall have to think of some excuse tomorrow as to why we are going out to luncheon."

"Am I really to be invited with you to Marlborough House?" questioned Lanthia breathlessly. "Would it not be wiser to say that I had a cold and for you to have luncheon alone with His Royal Highness?"

"I think as you were looking perfectly healthy this evening when he spoke with you, he would think it rather strange that you developed a cold so quickly!"

The Marquis was silent for a moment and then he added,

"It is no use running away from the mess we are in and I think it is better to face the music bravely."

"Just as you would face a dust storm in the desert or an avalanche on the mountains!"

The Marquis chuckled.

"Very well," he agreed, "and because we are fellow explorers, Lanthia, that is exactly what we must do. And tomorrow I will try and be as intelligent as Richard Burton would be about it."

"I am sure you will be as successful as him – he has never failed yet."

"That is true," admitted the Marquis, "and as he has survived, so shall we."

He rose to his feet.

Now he stood looking at her, thinking how lovely she looked in her pretty white dress.

Because she was so young and life was so exciting she seemed to vibrate almost as though a light was shining through her.

Then he told himself he was being imaginative and the sooner he left the better.

He held out his hand.

"Goodnight, Lanthia, and thank you more than I can possible say for all your kindness to me and the help you have given me."

She put her hand into his and the Marquis raised it to his lips.

As he did so he thought that actually, if she was not so young, he would have kissed her and it was what any other woman would have expected from him.

Strangely enough, there was not the expression in her eyes that he was accustomed to recognising, nor did she move instinctively nearer to him.

"What time will you be collecting me tomorrow?" she asked.

"At half-past twelve. Are you quite certain you can explain what is happening to your chaperone?"

"I will manage it somehow!"

Then as the Marquis reached the door she gave out a little cry.

"Wait!" she called.

"What is it, Lanthia?"

"I think it would be wise if I looked up the corridor just to see if that horrible man is waiting for you. He might consider it an opportunity of injuring you if he thought you were here. I am sure he carries a stiletto!"

The Marquis laughed.

"I think it a bit unlikely. At the same time it would be wise and sensible of you to see if the coast is clear for me."

Lanthia walked to the door and opened it.

She moved a few steps to the corner of the corridor. The gas lamps were still alight and there was no one to be seen. So she turned back.

"I think you are quite safe," she whispered, "but do hurry!"

"I will certainly do so and goodnight, Lanthia. As you must be aware you have been really wonderful."

He set off down the corridor walking swiftly.

Lanthia watched him for a moment and then turned back into her sitting room.

She was thinking how extraordinary it was that the Marquis was an explorer. Because he was so smart and so handsome, she thought he was what her father would have called 'a man about town' and was seldom seen outside London.

But he had actually journeyed to Tibet.

She could hardly believe it. Tibet was where her father had always wanted to go, but had reached no further than Nepal and on another trip he had spent some time in the Ural Mountains.

'I must tell Papa about the Marquis,' she decided as she undressed.

But then she wondered what her father and mother would say when they learnt that she had pretended to be engaged to him.

And that she had attended a dinner party with him tonight and would be accompanying him to a luncheon at Marlborough House tomorrow.

It all seemed just like one of her dreams and she could not believe that her involvement was wrong in any way.

Yet she *was* involved, because the Marquis had told an outright lie and she had accepted her part in maintaining his deception.

She realised that poor Mrs. Blossom had no idea what she was doing and there would therefore be no need for her to tell anyone that she had ever dined with the Duke of Sutherland at *The Langham*.

Nor that she had been taken to a dinner party by a man whom she had never met until he burst suddenly into her sitting room!

But now that the Spaniard had told the Prince of Wales they were engaged, things were very different.

She had even been asked to Marlborough House for luncheon and she could hardly pretend that it had happened quite casually.

How could she keep it all a secret from her parents, if the Prince of Wales was present at the Lord Lieutenant's ball.

He would undoubtedly speak to her and before he did so she would have to explain to her parents how she had met him.

'It is all becoming too complicated,' she thought, 'and I wish Mama was here to sort out the whole puzzle for me.'

When she finally climbed into her bed she was still thinking of what she should say to Mrs. Blossom and more importantly, what she should say when she returned home.

There was no doubt that the Marquis was extremely popular.

As they had walked around the dining room when dinner was over, everyone present had seemed pleased to see him.

"Hello, Rake," most of the gentlemen had called to him, followed by, "I thought I should see you here. What are you up to? Or is that an indiscreet question?"

They laughed as if they had made a good joke and the Marquis had made some light reply.

It all seemed in Lanthia's recollection so very much more vivid than any of her most outlandish dreams.

The brilliance of the dining room was unreal and so were the glamorous ladies glittering with diamonds, rubies and emeralds in their hair and round their necks.

And there was the Prince of Wales himself sitting beside the beautiful Lillie Langtry.

'I cannot really believe I am really seeing this,' she had said to herself.

When she looked at the Marquis, she felt that he too was not really human. He was a hero who had stepped out of one of the novels which her mother had said she was too young to read before she was eighteen.

'It was real, it really was!' Lanthia now told herself as she turned over on her pillow.

Then once again she imagined she was listening to the music being played in the hotel courtyard, until she fell asleep.

*

She woke early in the morning and dressed before she went into Mrs. Blossom's room to see how she was.

She expected that she would come into the sitting room as they had agreed they would have breakfast at eight o'clock.

However, when she entered Mrs. Blossom's room, it was in darkness.

She thought she was fast asleep until a husky voice from the bed asked,

"Is that you, Lanthia?"

"Yes it is. I do hope you had a good night."

"I am afraid, my dear, that I do believe I have now contracted a touch of influenza. I started to cough in the night and, although I took some pills, I know that I have a temperature, so I really should stay in bed."

"Of course you must," exclaimed Lanthia. "I will order you some breakfast, because I am sure you will feel better if you have a cup of coffee or some tea, but you must not get up."

"But what about you, Lanthia?"

"I shall be fine. I will engage a Hackney Carriage to the shop and arrange for it to wait while I have a fitting for my gown and then I will come back to the hotel."

"You do not think you should ask one of the maids to go with you?" suggested Mrs. Blossom.

"I shall be quite all right. Mama would not like me to walk about the streets alone, but if I go in a carriage and come back in one, there should be no harm in that."

"I suppose not," agreed Mrs. Blossom in a worried

tone. "Please, my dear, stay in your room as much as you can, I am sure I shall be better tomorrow."

"You do not think you should see a doctor?"

"No, of course not. I am not as bad as that. I have had these attacks before and if I take the right pills, it will all be over in twenty-four hours."

She spoke optimistically, but as Lanthia drew back the curtains she saw that the older woman looked pale and rather drawn.

She did everything she could, tidying the room and ordering breakfast.

Mrs. Blossom promised to try to eat something, but Lanthia knew at once that all she really wanted was to be able to rest and if possible sleep.

Her condition certainly made matters much easier as far as she was concerned and she fervently hoped that Mrs. Blossom would not realise that she had gone out to luncheon.

As soon as she had finished her breakfast she went downstairs and as she promised Mrs. Blossom, she took a Hackney Carriage to the shop where her evening gown was to be fitted.

She told the driver to wait to take her back to the hotel.

A great deal of work had been done since she had chosen the dress yesterday. In fact the *vendeuse* said it would be ready in two hours time.

Lanthia had the sudden idea that the Marquis might want her to dine with him tonight. If so, she had nothing elegant to wear except the gown she had worn last night.

There were two other gowns that she had hesitated over before she chose the one that was being altered.

She felt she must not let the Marquis down if they had to go to another party tonight, so she therefore bought both dresses hoping that her father would not be annoyed at the expense.

They were both up-to-date and not to be compared in any way with the simple dresses she had brought to wear when she was alone with Mrs. Blossom.

It was fortunate that yesterday she had bought a day dress, which she considered very pretty and the second one she had chosen had already been altered.

She could take it back with her now.

'At least I shall be correctly dressed for the lavish occasion at Marlborough House,' she thought.

The dress she was trying on was very becoming. It was the pale blue of forget-me-nots and accentuated the perfection of her skin and the gold of her hair.

It was a young girl's dress, but at the same time it was fashionable enough to compete with anything an older and more sophisticated woman would be wearing.

*

In one of the pretty hats she had bought yesterday, Lanthia waited patiently until just before half-past twelve for the Marquis.

She had called in to see Mrs. Blossom on her return from the shop and when she entered the room she saw that her chaperone was fast asleep.

Lanthia rather suspected she had taken a little more of the laudanum than she should and anyway it prevented her from asking any awkward questions.

When she realised that there was nothing more she could do, Lanthia walked back to the sitting room.

She rather expected that the Marquis might send a message saying he was waiting for her downstairs.

Instead, as she had left the door of the sitting room ajar, he walked straight in.

"Good morning, Lanthia," he called cheerily and as he spoke he was looking at her critically.

On his way to *The Langham* he had wondered if, in fact, Lanthia would look correctly dressed for Marlborough House.

He now vaguely remembered that she had not been looking particularly smart yesterday when he had burst into her sitting room to save himself from the Conté, although she had certainly looked lovely and perfectly gowned last night.

In his long experience of women he often found that while at night they 'got away with it,' so to speak, in the daytime they made lamentable mistakes.

Especially if they were not really a member of what was known as the *Beau Monde*.

But Lanthia in her blue gown and smart little hat looked exactly as if she had stepped out of a picture book.

Or, as the Marquis said to himself, 'a fairy tale.'

He had retired to bed last night thinking she was without exception the loveliest girl he had ever seen.

In the morning light he had felt more cynical, as he could not help wondering if it was just because she had saved him by being so obliging, that he had found her so exceptional.

Perhaps on closer inspection today he might be a little disappointed.

He was, in fact, although he would not admit it to himself, feeling rather nervous about their visit today to Marlborough House.

He knew the Spaniard had, out of sheer spite, told the Prince of Wales he was secretly engaged.

Firstly, because he had asked him to keep it a secret.

Secondly, because he knew that the Prince of Wales

would be annoyed at anyone hearing a secret about one of his special friends before it was told to him.

Thirdly, if the Conté still suspected it was untrue, then the Marquis would undoubtedly find himself in deep trouble and would receive a Royal rebuke.

All this flashed through the Marquis's mind and he enquired,

"Is everything all right? What of your chaperone? What have you told her?"

"She is in bed with a high temperature and at the moment fast asleep."

"That is surely lucky for us," he exclaimed. "Once again the Gods are on our side!"

"We must hope so, but I am somewhat concerned about what you will say when you have to tell everybody I have gone back to the country and it is unlikely we shall ever see each other again!"

The Marquis smiled.

"I shall merely recount, dolefully, that you thought I was too frivolous and far too interested in other women to make you a good husband. You therefore have thrown me over and of course I am broken-hearted!"

The way he spoke made Lanthia laugh.

"Now you are just making it a fairy tale," she said, "and I have a feeling no one will believe you."

"They will if I tell them the story convincingly and, naturally, to assuage my dismay at being thrown over by you, I can explore a part of the world I have not been to before!"

"Oh, that is most unfair!"

"Why?" enquired the Marquis.

"Because it will be wonderful for you, while I shall

be left behind to imagine I am exploring somewhere no one has ever ventured, as I ride through the woods."

"Why the woods, Lanthia?"

"Because that is where I always tell myself a story and I do so in my mind what you actually achieve with your whole being."

She gave a deep sigh.

"Oh, *why* was I not born a man?"

The Marquis looked at her quizzically and realised she was speaking sincerely.

"I think that a great number of men in your life, Lanthia, will be only too delighted you have been born a woman and think how amusing it will be when you have them at your feet, begging you for just one kind word or even a consoling kiss because you have refused to marry them."

He was now saying the first words that came into his head.

Then, as if she had taken him seriously, she replied,

"I have met very few men in Huntingdonshire, for we have been in mourning for a year for my grandfather and that has seemed a very long time."

"Well, now I am taking you out for luncheon and I am sure you will meet at least two or three men, but they may not all be unattached."

Lanthia quickly looked at the clock.

"We must not be late."

"No, of course not, now come along – my chaise is outside and I have an idea that you would like to look at my horses."

Lanthia's eyes lit up.

"Have you some really good stallions?"

"I shall be quite annoyed if you don't think so and incidentally, while you were talking about your horses last night, I omitted to tell you that at this very moment my horse is the favourite for the Gold Cup."

Lanthia clapped her hands.

"That is just *so* exciting! Oh, please, please can I see him before I have to go away and pretend I have never met you?"

"I am sure that can be arranged."

They went downstairs to find the Marquis's chaise drawn up in front of the entrance.

He expected Lanthia to climb in, but first she ran to the horses' heads.

She thoroughly inspected the pair he was driving before she finally got into the chaise.

"You are quite right, they are magnificent animals and you must be very proud of them."

"They are my new acquisitions, but I have in the stables a team of four I would like you to see, because they are perfectly matched and look very impressive in front of my Travelling Carriage."

Lanthia did not say anything.

After a moment as they were driving down Regent Street, the Marquis asked,

"What are you thinking about?"

"I was only thinking, as I did last night, how very different you are from what I expected."

"You mean because I am an explorer and because I love horses."

"Yes, both those things, and I am rather surprised I did not realise at once that you are not just what Papa calls 'a man about town'."

"I should be most insulted," asserted the Marquis, "if anyone thought I had no other interests."

"I don't want to be rude," said Lanthia hesitantly, "but it is because you do not look like an explorer!"

"What do explorers look like?"

"Like pictures I have seen of Mr. Richard Burton or they have long beards and rugged faces and of course their skin has been burned by the blazing sun until they hardly look like a white man."

The Marquis chuckled.

"I think you must have been reading too many story books. Explorers today travel far more comfortably than in the past. Even so I have had my moments, when I have either been dripping with heat or freezing with cold."

"That is just what I want you to tell me all about. I do wish we did not have to go to this luncheon party and make polite conversation."

The Marquis was amused.

He could not think of any other woman who would not be in ecstatic raptures at the idea of having luncheon at Marlborough House with the Prince of Wales.

Yet he felt at once Lanthia was sincere in preferring to hear about the discomforts that everyone endured if they were exploring in an unknown part of the world.

He could remember many moments when he had been desperately uncomfortable and at other times when he thought that the last moment of his life had come and it would be impossible to save himself.

Yet he had survived.

He had to acknowledge that while he relished every difficulty and danger of the unknown, he also enjoyed the comforts and luxuries with which he could indulge himself at home.

Especially when he could enjoy them with someone soft and beautiful, who could ignite in him a burning fire as the Contessa had succeeded in doing yesterday.

There was no doubt that she was a past master at exciting a man physically.

He would have been untruthful if he said he had not enjoyed every moment of the time he had spent with her and he had only himself to blame for having taken such a ridiculous risk.

He therefore harboured no wish for this pretty child beside him to suffer any further because of his stupidity.

Of course he had been so idiotic not to make sure, knowing his reputation, that the Conté would not return to the hotel earlier than his wife expected, as it was the sort of thing he would do, simply because he wished to take her unawares.

The Conté might be laughed at for his jealousy, but the Marquis knew he had good reason for it.

He was obviously not the first man the Contessa had captivated with her green eyes and seductive voice.

Now having made such a fundamental mistake, the Marquis knew that he had to extract himself and, of course, Lanthia, from what could become an embarrassing disaster.

Now he had discovered who she was, the Marquis had an uncomfortable feeling that Sir Philip Grenville and his wife might insist on his saving her good name.

To put it simply, they would put pressure on him to offer her marriage.

'She is pretty, amusing, and quite unlike any other girl I have ever met,' the Marquis thought as he drove on. 'At the same time I refuse to be married and nothing and nobody will force me to do so!'

Lanthia was quietly observing his driving and felt

that he was most definitely an expert and she knew that she would have nothing in common with any man who did not love horses and who could not manage them.

Her father had always been an outstanding rider and she herself had ridden almost as soon as she could crawl.

She was thinking that the Marquis must be a good judge of horseflesh to have chosen the pair he was driving and also to have a favourite running at Ascot.

'He is so very good-looking,' she told herself. 'But there is something about him which makes me feel as if there is a barrier between us.'

Then she realised what it was – it was his revulsion and fear of being married.

Although they were only pretending to be engaged, even that made him want to shy away from her as a horse might do.

'He is perfectly safe,' she told herself. 'If he thinks that I am going to fall in love with him, he is very much mistaken!'

Last night at dinner she had not missed the number of ladies who had spoken to him in a way that told her that they found him very, very attractive.

When she saw the Contessa looking at him it was quite obvious what she felt for him and perhaps the Conté was right in thinking he had indeed made love to her.

The Contessa had been far too clever last night to attempt to speak directly to the Marquis and yet she could not prevent herself from looking at him from time to time.

Innocently Lanthia had intercepted her glances and if the Marquis was really convinced that the Contessa had something tigerish about her, she had felt the same.

She could almost feel the Contessa reaching out to the Marquis, her hands like claws seeking to clutch him.

Lanthia thought she was definitely eerie and rather frightening and this opinion helped her to understand to some extent why the Marquis should be running away from the idea of marriage.

Any woman who became his wife would be much too possessive. She would attempt to imprison him just as he wanted to go exploring and needed to be free.

'I understand,' she thought, 'I do understand and I would like to tell him that he need not be afraid of me.'

She knew, however, it was something she could not say.

It was with a flourish that the Marquis drew up his horses outside Marlborough House.

The groom, who had been sitting up behind, took the reins from him and he and Lanthia stepped out.

Once again she felt she was walking into a sublime dream.

They were greeted in the entrance hall by a Scottish ghillie in Highland dress and a scarlet-coated footman with a powdered wig took the Marquis's hat and gloves.

A butler then escorted them to a sitting room where Princess Alexandra was waiting to receive them.

As she held out her hand in delight to the Marquis, she looked so beautiful that Lanthia thought,

'I know I am dreaming. I only hope I do not wake up too soon!'

CHAPTER FIVE

Ever since she had been small Lanthia had heard so much about Alexandra, the Princess of Wales.

As she became older she began to realise that Her Royal Highness was completely adored and idolised by the whole country. She was just so beautiful, pure, radiant and gracious that the public considered her their fairy Princess.

Because Lanthia had lived a very cloistered life in the country, she had no idea of what the Marquis and many others in the know understood only too well.

It was that Princess Alexandra had won for herself a popularity never previously accorded to a Royal Consort, a great deal of it being due to the fact that the Prince of Wales was known to be unfaithful.

As Lanthia swept to the floor in a deep curtsy, she thought that, as she had once read, that the Princess looked like 'a fairy doll on top of England's Christmas Tree'.

The Prince came forward to greet her saying,

"You are now looking even prettier than last night, Miss Grenville!"

Lanthia smiled at him and the Prince introduced her to his other guests.

To her rapt surprise among them were Mr. and Mrs. William Gladstone. He had been Britain's Prime Minister until Mr. Benjamin Disraeli had superseded him.

However, Lanthia had read in the newspapers that there was every likelihood of Mr. Gladstone coming back again with the Liberals winning the next election.

A number of people thought it very strange that the Gladstones should be such close friends of the Prince and Princess of Wales as it was well known that the Queen had a strong dislike for him while he was Prime Minister.

What very few people realised was that the Princess preferred as her guests, those gentlemen who actually 'did' something, such as politicians, Churchmen and musicians.

This had meant that Sir Arthur Sullivan and Signor Tosti were very regular visitors at Marlborough House and although most of the aristocratic families adored Princess Alexandra, their interests were very different from hers.

She had confided to one of her close friends that the conversation of the British 'upper crust' always involved killing things, such as birds and wild animals, but where she was concerned, she preferred life and happiness.

The Prince next introduced Lanthia to Mr. Oliver Montagu, who her father had often talked about.

He was the Equerry in attendance on the Princess – he was always at her side to protect and serve her in a way that many people found touching.

Among several other guests that Lanthia met was Lord Hardwicke.

The Marquis knew and decided to tell Lanthia later that, because the Prince was so fussy about his appearance, he had introduced a number of fashion innovations of his own.

A short navy-blue jacket was adopted for dinner by his whole entourage as well as all ship's Officers and when the Prince appeared wearing gloves with black stitching, all the young gentlemen in White's were quick to imitate him.

His friends all wanted to please him and so Lord Hardwicke had inspired his hat-maker to produce what the Marlborough House set acclaimed as a 'perfect topper.'

As the guests eventually all sat down to luncheon, Lanthia felt everything was so informal that it was difficult to believe she was actually in the Royal Household.

The Marquis, although Lanthia had no idea he was doing so, was watching her carefully.

It was not only to see that she did nothing wrong, but he was really wondering what would be her reaction at finding herself sitting down to a meal with the Prince and Princess of Wales.

Princess Alexandra had indeed managed to capture the hearts of the British people when, despite her beauty, all the odds might have been against it.

Queen Victoria had been only too well aware from the example of the behaviour of her uncle, King William IV, that her family were extremely hot-blooded.

She had been faced with the problem of finding a suitable wife for her eldest son, who would surely inherit this characteristic.

The Court was astounded when she selected a little known Danish Princess, a choice which from the political point of view was extremely embarrassing.

But Alexandra was, however, undoubtedly the most beautiful Princess in the whole of Europe and at eighteen she became the perfect wife for a somewhat over-vigorous young man of twenty.

That the Prince at once fell madly in love with her was a justification of his mother's choice.

Yet there was no doubt that the Queen thoroughly disapproved of many of their friends, their parties and the manner in which they lived.

On one occasion she commented with disapproval that Alexandra had all her five children in the room when she was writing letters and no nurse in attendance. In fact she and the Prince allowed their children to climb over and around them like puppies.

The Princess went even further. When she could, she would go to the nursery, put on a flannel apron and bathe the children herself. Then she would rock them to sleep in their little beds.

It was all a question of being young, energetic and living life to the full.

Yet what no one could understand, as the Marquis knew only too well, was that when the public realised the Prince was being unfaithful, Alexandra never complained nor appeared to be in any way upset by him.

Whether she was or was not in private, no one ever knew.

It was Oliver Montagu who kept her from being talked about and he made sure that she could not be harmed by any gossip leaking from their home.

Looking closely at the Princess across the table, the Marquis could see that naturally she had changed during the seventeen years of her marriage.

Yet Alexandra was surely still incredibly beautiful, but she was obviously no longer as mobile as the young bride of 1863.

Rheumatic fever had left her with a stiff knee and this prevented her from skating on the Sandringham ponds or dancing in the ballroom.

But she was still graceful and still had a radiant smile which seemed to welcome everyone.

And she was apparently still extremely happy with her husband.

The Prince had always treated her with the greatest kindness and respect and even his closest friends had never heard him complain at her frequent unpunctuality.

The Marquis knew, because he was so often with the Prince, that he was always watchful to see that every respect was shown to his wife.

He had been a guest at the time when the Duchess of Marlborough attended a dinner in their honour and wore a diamond crescent instead of the traditional tiara.

The Prince of Wales had looked disapprovingly at her and then he said,

"The Princess has taken the trouble to wear a tiara. Why have you not done so?"

The Duchess had been embarrassed and needless to say the story had flown round the town, but the Marquis had thought the Prince was definitely in the right.

It had been a special honour at this luncheon party that Lanthia should be seated on the Prince's left with Mrs. Gladstone on his right.

Watching them across the table the Marquis saw Lanthia chatting away in her usual enthusiastic manner.

She was making the Prince laugh and he wondered how many young girls of her age would have been so self-composed.

Then he considered that maybe Princess Alexandra had been the same when she had first arrived in England to marry an unknown Prince whom she had never met.

She must have been a vision of loveliness just as, he considered, Lanthia was now.

It struck him that in many ways the two women resembled each other. They each had large blue eyes set in a heart-shaped face and their hair was like gold.

Then as he continued seeking resemblances he was aware again that the Princess was undoubtedly beginning to look a little older and he knew she was having difficulty in hearing what people said.

The Prince was laughing once again at something Lanthia had said to him.

The Marquis noticed a certain glitter in His Royal Highness's eyes which made him stiffen.

He recognised all too well what that meant.

In his friendship with the Prince he had known it was always a danger signal to any woman to whom His Royal Highness was talking.

Quite unexpectedly the Marquis felt angry.

Last night, because he knew the Prince so well, he had suspected that his passion for Lillie Langtry was now on the wane.

It was nothing he could put into words and yet he was aware, as if the Prince had told him, that the writing was on the wall.

Another passionate liaison between him and a great beauty was clearly coming to an end.

What the Marquis had never expected was that in inviting Lanthia to luncheon, the Prince meant something more than that he was anxious to show his affection for an old friend.

Yet there was now no doubt from the way he was looking at Lanthia that he found her entrancing.

It was with difficulty that the Marquis did not rise and take Lanthia away at once.

He had seen so many women succumb to the Prince as if he was a tidal wave they could not resist. The mere fact that he was even near to them would start their hearts beating faster.

Then he told himself he was being absurd.

How could the Prince ever consider Lanthia to be anything other than a young, unsophisticated and innocent girl and she was engaged, as far as he knew, to be married to one of his closest friends.

At the same time he was well aware that the Prince did not bother with any conventions, rules or gentlemanly code of behaviour when it concerned his heart.

He always found a beautiful woman irresistible and when he did so there were no barriers he was not prepared to break down. In fact there were no steps he would not take to capture her.

'It would be a crime against nature itself to let that happen,' the Marquis decided, 'where young Lanthia is concerned.'

He appreciated that she had found everything they had done since he first met her part of her dream world and there had quite obviously been no reality at all about their encounter.

But she would find it very real indeed if the Prince started to make advances towards her.

Which, the Marquis now suspected, was already in his mind.

'I will not allow it!' he fumed and wondered what on earth he could do to could prevent it.

The dishes provided for the guests at Marlborough House were invariably delicious, but the meals were never long drawn out affairs.

As soon as they had finished the dessert course, the Princess took the ladies back into the sitting room.

Lanthia had hardly looked at the room earlier and she now saw that it was heavily panelled with the sofas and easy chairs upholstered in leather of the same colour as the rich blue velvet curtains.

There was a large writing desk which she guessed was used by the Prince and it was close to a table strewn with documents, reference books and newspapers.

There were two dogs lying on the rug in front of the fireplace and in the fashion set by the Queen at Windsor Castle there were enormous displays of family photographs everywhere.

But Lanthia only had a little time to look round.

As soon as the gentlemen had joined them from the dining room, the Marquis proposed that they should leave.

Lanthia was reluctant to do so, but she rose to her feet obediently, feeling as she did so that the Gladstones had settled down to stay for a much longer time.

She said her goodbyes to the Princess, curtsied and thanked her for inviting her to luncheon.

"It has most certainly been, Your Royal Highness, a wonderful experience which I shall always remember."

"You must come again," said Princess Alexandra, "the Prince and I are always glad to meet any friends of Rake's."

She smiled at the Marquis and he kissed her hand.

"You have always been so very kind to me, ma'am, and one day perhaps I shall be able to repay you."

He was ruminating that he was doing so already in taking Lanthia away!

His suspicions aroused at luncheon were increased when the Prince walked with them to the top of the stairs.

"I have found Lanthia even more enchanting that I did last night, Rake," he confided. "We must fix up a little dinner party before the end of the week when I can see you both again."

"What can I say, sir, except that I am very grateful to you."

He could not, however, repress a touch of sharpness in his voice, as he was well aware that the Prince was not listening to him, but kept his eyes on Lanthia.

She was certainly the loveliest sight for anyone to behold.

The Marquis took his hat from one of the footmen and noticed that the Prince had not returned to the sitting room, but was watching them quizzically from behind a Chinese screen.

He pretended that he did not see him as he followed Lanthia through the door and they waited while his chaise drew up in front of them.

They climbed in and as they were driving away, Lanthia said,

"Thank you, thank you so much for taking me to Marlborough House. It was really a wonderful occasion I shall always remember."

"And doubtless the Prince will remember you too!" the Marquis murmured.

Lanthia gave a little laugh.

"I think that is extremely unlikely, but he is very interesting and it was a great privilege for me to sit next to him at luncheon."

"I thought you might find the occasion rather dull with everyone so much older than you."

"I thought all the guests were fascinating including Mr. Gladstone."

"At your age," the Marquis now remarked, driving carefully through the bustling traffic, "you should be with young gentlemen and finding yourself a suitable husband."

Lanthia grinned.

"Now you are sounding like my mother and that is what she will expect me to do when we come up to London next month."

"It is what I hope you will do too. You are so very beautiful, Lanthia, and there will be plenty of young men who will be eager to marry you."

"I have no wish to be married until I find exactly the right person," insisted Lanthia.

"What do you think he will be like?"

Lanthia was silent for a while and then she replied as if she was thinking out her answer very carefully,

"I am not exactly sure what he will look like, but I will know at once when I meet him that he is the one man I am looking for."

The Marquis considered this to be a rather strange answer.

After passing a carriage that was going very slowly in front of him, he enquired,

"Who are you looking for exactly? Someone with an important title?"

Lanthia smiled.

"No, of course not! Someone who will understand me and what I am thinking."

"Is that so very difficult? And naturally, like every other young woman, you hope to wear a coronet on your head and throw large parties like the Duke of Sutherland's last night."

There was a cynical note in his voice.

"That is *not* what I want!" she asserted positively. "I want something *very* different."

"I don't believe you. You are just trying to make it sound more difficult than it really is!"

Lanthia did not answer and after a moment he said,

"Supposing, now just supposing, that someone like me asked you to be my wife, what would you say?"

Lanthia did not hesitate.

"I would say *no*. Although it would be very kind of you to think of it."

The Marquis was astonished.

He had expected her, as he had mentioned himself, to look coy or perhaps shy and avoid the question.

Because he could not help being curious, he asked her,

"Why would you refuse me?"

"It is rather difficult to put into words, but there is something missing."

The Marquis turned his head to look at her in sheer amazement.

"In me?" he questioned.

Lanthia nodded.

"I cannot really explain it, but I shall never be able to say 'yes' to any man until I am convinced that he is the one who is with me in my dreams."

The Marquis could not think of any answer to her.

In fact he was completely astounded.

He was so used to women clinging onto him and falling into his arms. They would look at him passionately almost before he was even introduced to them.

He could not believe that Lanthia had actually said she would not marry him even if he asked her to do so.

It was naturally something he had no intention of doing.

Equally how was it possible that she was the only woman in the world he had ever met who did not desire him as her husband or lover?

'I must be growing old,' he pondered to himself, 'and perhaps I am losing my attractions!'

At the same time he could see the fire glowing in the Contessa's eyes yesterday and the same familiar flicker was very present in the eyes of several of the ladies he had spoken to at the Duke's dinner party.

This young girl from the country had been with him in the most unusual circumstances during the last twenty-four hours.

Yet she had told him quite firmly and truthfully that something was *missing* in him.

'I just do not understand,' mused the Marquis.

He drove on further and as they proceeded down Regent Street he was aware that Lanthia was looking at the shops with delight.

She was obviously completely unaware that she had dropped a bombshell at his feet.

As they neared *The Langham*, the Marquis said,

"I am afraid I cannot ask you out to dinner tonight as I have a long-standing engagement with some friends at White's Club."

"It was very kind of you to take me to luncheon at Marlborough House and I enjoyed it all enormously," she replied, hiding her disappointment.

"We will have luncheon tomorrow," suggested the Marquis, "and I will try to find out, perhaps tonight, how long the Conté is staying at the hotel. As soon as he leaves we will no longer need to be scared of him and what he might do to me next."

"I too must return home to the country perhaps the day after tomorrow."

"We can only hope that nothing untoward happens before then, but we must make our plans tomorrow as to what we shall say and what we shall do if the Conté has talked to any more people."

"Do you think His Royal Highness will talk?"

"I managed to have a word with him before we left the dining room," answered the Marquis, "and he promised to keep our engagement a secret."

"Then I am sure he will keep his word," she said confidently.

The Marquis drew up outside *The Langham*.

"Thank you for a lovely time," Lanthia said again.

She smiled at him and when a porter opened the carriage door, she stepped out of the chaise.

She waved her hand and the Marquis raised his hat.

Then as he drove off, she walked up the steps and into the entrance hall.

The manager was standing just inside.

"Did you have a nice luncheon, Miss Grenville?" he enquired.

"I have had such a wonderful time," replied Lanthia dreamily.

"I hope everything is to your satisfaction here in the hotel?"

"We are very comfortable and I enjoyed the party last night enormously."

"I guessed that you would," answered the manager.

Lanthia walked towards the lift, thinking that she had perhaps been a little extravagant in buying the extra evening dresses.

Unless of course the Marquis should take her out again tomorrow night.

'It must be so boring for him to be hampered with me,' she told herself in the lift. 'And I still cannot believe I have really had luncheon at Marlborough House with the Prince and Princess of Wales. It is a pity I cannot tell Mrs. Blossom about it all and I must ask the Marquis first before I let anyone into the secret.'

*

The Marquis drove away from *The Langham*.

He realised that Lanthia was disappointed that he was not taking her out to dinner tonight.

It was something he would have liked to do, but he had, however, thought it was a mistake to be seen in public with her.

It would undoubtedly mean more people would be talking about them than there were already.

He hoped that although they had both been at the Duke's party last night, no one except the Spaniards and the Prince of Wales would connect them with each other.

He believed that the Prince would keep his promise not to tell anyone that they were engaged.

'Lanthia has behaved so extremely well in the most difficult circumstances,' he murmured to himself.

It now occurred to him that he should have sent her flowers as he would always have done automatically with any other woman.

As she was so young and their relationship with each other so completely different, he had not thought of it.

Now as he had nothing else to do, he drove to Bond Street to a flower shop where his secretary bought some of the flowers that decorated his house in Park Lane.

As he entered the flower shop, the proprietor bowed respectfully and asked what he could do for him.

"I am seeking something unusual," he replied.

He looked around and noticed a basket filled with pink rosebuds not yet in bloom. They were most skilfully arranged with bows of pink ribbon tied onto the basket.

"I will take that," he said.

The shopkeeper hurriedly wrapped up the bottom of the basket and carried it out to the chaise.

The Marquis was just about to climb back into the

driving seat when he saw that the shop next door was the jeweller his mother and some of his relations patronised.

He remembered his father had said he brought his mother's engagement ring there and he also gave her an expensive present from the same shop every Christmas and on her birthday.

The Marquis decided that he should buy something attractive to thank Lanthia for everything she had done for him.

He was welcomed by the manager and shown into his private room.

"What can I do for you, my Lord?" he intoned.

"I want something not too flamboyant but pretty for a very young lady," answered the Marquis. "In fact she is a *debutante*, so it should not be at all flashy."

"No, of course not, my Lord," the manager replied, as if the Marquis had reproached him for even thinking of such an idea.

He snapped his fingers and an attendant hurried to find what he thought was most appropriate.

While he was doing so the manager said,

"That reminds me, my Lord, we have just finished mending the clasp of the magnificent brooch that your aunt – the Countess – wore at the ball the other night. She told me it should be repaired as it would be a tragedy if it was lost."

The Marquis was listening to him although he was not particularly interested.

The manager took a small jewel case from a drawer and the Marquis saw that it was stamped in gold with his family crest.

He recognised at once that the piece belonged to the famous Rakecliffe jewels that had been handed down for many generations and were considered by the cognoscenti to be the most outstanding collection in private hands.

As one of his relations had remarked only the other day,

"Apart from the Royal jewels there is no other to compare to ours."

The Marquis had agreed with her that they were in fact unique.

His great-grandfather had brought a great number of gems from India and had arranged for them to be set by the finest jeweller in Paris.

The result was the equal of anything that could be worn by Princess Alexandra and the many necklaces which comprised every known jewel were outstanding.

The manager was now showing him an enormous brooch in the centre of which was a very large diamond in the shape of a star and the diamonds which framed it were all perfect.

It was so unusual that it was impossible to have it adequately valued for insurance purposes.

The brooch had been cleaned while being mended and in consequence it was shining like a star that had fallen down from the sky.

The Marquis took it out from its velvet case and turned it over.

"I can see you have made a good job of it," he said, "and it would be a tragedy indeed if it was lost."

"It certainly would, my Lord, so I was wondering, whether you could take it with you. I find it difficult to decide how I can return it to Park Lane without there being a risk of it being lost or stolen on the way."

The Marquis smiled.

"I cannot believe London is quite as bad as that, but I should be very upset if it went missing."

He put the case in his pocket.

Then he started to look at the pieces the manager was showing him as a present for Lanthia.

He knew it was incorrect for a young girl to accept anything of value from a gentleman unless she was actually going to marry him.

As Lanthia had said quite clearly that she would not marry him even if he asked her, that question did not arise.

He was still finding it extraordinary that she should have said 'no' so quickly, without even considering it.

Finally, he chose a very pretty bracelet exquisitely made in blue enamel with a small charm falling from it on which was written *good luck*.

The manager placed it into a velvet jewel box and would have wrapped it up if the Marquis had not stopped him from doing so.

He also put the box in his pocket.

He was planning to present it to Lanthia tomorrow when they had luncheon together.

Then as he went back to his chaise he remembered the flowers.

By now it was late in the afternoon and he knew there would be a number of letters for him to sign at home.

Therefore he decided that the best thing would be for him to leave the flowers until he went out to dinner.

It would not be too much of a detour to stop at *The Langham* even if he was heading for St. James's Street.

It would take too long now to drive there and then back to Park Lane, so the Marquis returned to his house.

He found, as he expected, there was a huge pile of letters waiting for him on his desk. Some of them needed signing and when he had done so he pushed them on one side for his secretary to deal with tomorrow morning.

The other letters were private and his secretary was far too discreet and too discerning to have opened any of them.

They were mostly written on pale-coloured writing paper and some gave off the faint scent of exotic perfume.

The Marquis turned them all over without opening even one of them.

Leaving them on his writing desk he now walked upstairs, thinking again of Lanthia and the way the Prince had looked at her.

'The sooner she does go back to the country, the better,' he thought. 'She is much too pretty and I have no wish to be responsible for her.'

Yet he knew, because she had saved him from the Conté, that was exactly what he now was.

Just how could he do anything else when she had behaved so bravely?

She had saved him from having to go at dawn and fight the Conté in Green Park and doubtless he would at this precise moment be nursing a badly shattered arm and wondering how he could avoid being forced into exile.

The Queen would undoubtedly order him out of the country.

'I can never be grateful enough to Lanthia,' mused the Marquis. 'She might have turned out to be some stupid woman, who would merely have screamed or fainted at the way the Conté behaved.'

It was most unfortunate that the Spaniard was still in London and still doubtless waiting for his revenge in one way or another.

He had already made as much trouble as possible and the Marquis, however, had the uneasy feeling he would not think it enough.

He would wish to go a great deal further before he was satisfied.

'I will try to find out just how long he is staying in London.'

He had always known that any piece of gossip or useful news was always available at White's.

As the Contessa was so beautiful, several members would doubtless have some information about her, whether it was complimentary or derogatory.

By the time the Marquis had walked downstairs, his closed carriage, which he always used at night, was waiting for him.

Most people used only one horse in the evening, but the Marquis liked to be the exception to every rule in having two.

Tonight his stallions were both perfectly matched and completely black except for white stars on their noses, and he paused for a second to gaze at them with a satisfied air as he climbed into the carriage.

On his instructions the flowers had been placed on the seat opposite him and he hoped as the horses moved off that they would please Lanthia.

He had with him the family brooch he had picked up from the jeweller and he intended to take it back to his house in the country when he next went there.

All the family jewellery was kept at his country seat because it was safer and he was in fact nervous of anything of great importance being kept in London at the moment.

There had been a series of burglaries in Park Lane and nearly everyone except for himself had lost either their jewels or their silver.

When he had changed his clothes this evening his valet had taken the brooch out of his coat pocket and had asked the Marquis where he wanted it put.

The Marquis had thought for a moment.

"I would say the safe," he replied. "But at the same time there have been so many burglaries, I would not want us to be the next victim."

"Oh, I hopes not, my Lord," his valet said.

"So do I, Hopkinson, so I will take the brooch with me."

He tucked it into the pocket of his evening jacket, thinking he would deposit it in the safe at White's Club until tomorrow.

There was always a large amount of money in that particular safe as so many card games were played for very high stakes by the Club members and he knew that every possible precaution was in place to prevent it from being pilfered.

In fact one of the most trusted and strong servants always slept in the same room as the safe.

The Marquis believed he was taking every possible precaution with the brooch that he and his family prized so highly.

One day he would expect the jewels would be worn by his wife when and if he ever had one.

He wondered what she would be like and then he could not help thinking of how lovely Lanthia had looked last night.

When she had stopped in the courtyard to look up at the water being thrown up by the fountain towards the sky, he thought she was breathtaking.

'She is stunningly beautiful,' he told himself, 'more beautiful than anyone I have ever seen.'

Once again he was aware of the glint he had seen in the Prince's eyes which had made him feel angry.

The Marquis's carriage came to a standstill and he realised that quicker than he had expected he was outside the hotel.

He picked up the basket of pink roses, stepped out and walked up the steps and into the entrance hall.

He thought it would be best to leave the basket with the porter to take upstairs to Lanthia.

He was sure she would not be going out tonight and his roses would therefore be a pleasant surprise for her.

The porter, who had been attending to a hotel guest, turned round as the Marquis put the basket down on the counter.

"Are you alright, my Lord?" he enquired. "We was upset when we heard you'd had an accident!"

"*An accident*?" repeated the Marquis, incredulous. "What are you talking about?"

"Miss Grenville was fetched, my Lord, because the boys said you'd had some accident and wanted her. She came rushing down here and went to where you was in a carriage which was waiting outside."

"I don't understand what you can be saying. I have had no accident. Who brought this message?"

The porter looked round.

"It were young Tommy, my Lord, who took the young boy upstairs to Miss Grenville."

"Call him," the Marquis ordered sharply. "I want to speak to him at once."

Even as he spoke he knew with a sinking heart that something was very wrong.

In fact he was convinced the Conté was striking at him again!

CHAPTER SIX

On her return to the hotel Lanthia went at once to see Mrs. Blossom, who was feeling a little better but still rather hazy.

Lanthia suspected she had been taking more of the laudanum.

It was obvious that she was not thinking of getting up or having dinner with her and from the way she spoke, Lanthia considered it most unlikely that she would want anything to eat.

"Is there anything I can do for you?" she asked.

"No, my dear, I am sure I shall be better tomorrow," Mrs. Blossom replied.

It was almost as if she was repeating something she had told herself she must say and her words did not sound very confident.

'At least,' Lanthia thought as she left her, 'I will not have to go home tomorrow, but can remain in London for another day.'

She realised, being completely honest with herself, that the reason she wanted to stay was so that she could be with the Marquis again.

Could anything be more exciting than everything that had happened to her so far?

It still seemed just incredible that she had dined last night with the Duke and Duchess of Sutherland and today had been taken to luncheon at Marlborough House.

'I am lucky, very lucky,' she thought. 'I only hope I will be able to tell Mama about all my adventures.'

She had already made up her mind about one matter – it would be a mistake to let Mrs. Blossom know anything about what had happened while she had been ill.

She would undoubtedly blame herself for not being a better chaperone.

Lanthia felt that she was being a little disloyal in thinking it was a relief not to have had to worry about her.

She went to her own bedroom.

Taking off the pretty blue dress she had worn at the luncheon, she hung it up in the wardrobe, which was filling rapidly with all her new dresses and gowns.

She looked at them and hoped that she would have a chance of wearing them all.

'I must not be greedy,' she decided. 'I have had so much already and I shall always remember how kind the Marquis has been to me.'

He had said that he too was grateful to her and she was not surprised.

She knew by the way the Conté had been staring at him last night that he really hated the Marquis in an almost fanatical way.

'Perhaps when I have gone away he will strike at him again,' she surmised, 'and then there will be no one to save him.'

However, she told herself she was being stupid.

Of course, seeing how tall and very strong he was, the Marquis could easily look after himself.

She could understand in a way why other men were jealous of him.

'Anyhow he must be so very careful,' she went on

thinking, 'although there cannot be many men around as spiteful and unpleasant as the Conté.'

As she was only going to dine alone, she put on one of her simple muslin dresses that she had brought with her to wear when she was alone with Mrs. Blossom.

She realised it was just impossible for her to dine downstairs by herself and therefore she must order dinner in her sitting room.

She was not at all hungry, having enjoyed such an excellent luncheon at Marlborough House and she thought she would read one of the books she had brought with her.

She had known, even if she was in London with so many exciting things to do like buying new clothes, there would still be time when she would want to read.

Lanthia had therefore brought two books from her father's library both written by famous explorers and she wished now she had brought one of Richard Burton's.

Then she remembered that the Marquis said he had travelled a great deal and he had not yet told her, as she wanted him to, about all his adventures.

She said a little prayer that she would indeed have a chance to hear about them before she left.

She wondered now why she had not asked him that afternoon which countries he had visited, as she could have easily done as they were driving away from Marlborough House.

But he had been talking about her and asking who she wanted to marry.

'I suppose,' she told herself, 'it was very rude of me to say that if he did ask me I would say 'no.' But I had to tell him the truth!'

Lanthia was thinking again about her dream man who always rode beside her in the woods and instinctively the thought made her yearn for fresh air and so she ran to the window.

She looked out onto Portland Place.

At the same time she was still feeling as if she was riding beneath the trees in the woods at home.

The sun was percolating through their broad leaves and someone was riding beside her.

Someone who understood that she was listening to the goblins working deep in the ground.

Someone who could see the nymphs hiding behind the trunks of the trees.

How could she explain to the Marquis or to anyone else the strange feelings she then harboured within her.

Nor would they understand that she was talking to the invisible man beside her, who felt the same as she did about everything.

'How can I marry *anyone*,' she asked herself, 'if I am always thinking about someone else, even though he is invisible.'

It was all too difficult to put into words, because, as she knew herself, it was not only what she was thinking but what she felt.

However she did not want the Marquis to think that she did not admire him.

Then she laughed out loud.

Was it likely to worry him one way or another?

He had so many beautiful women like the Contessa looking at him with longing in their eyes.

And he is most fortunate that he has a great number of friends such as the Duchess of Sutherland and Princess Alexandra.

'They are very fond of him as well and I know that

if Papa and Mama met him, they would like him too.'

Then she was wondering once again how she could tell her parents about all the extraordinary things that had happened to her since she came to London.

'If I read about it in a book, I should not believe it,' she thought. 'And yet I suppose the Marquis and Richard Burton have adventures like this every day when they are on their travels.'

She was trying to think what it would be like if she set out on an expedition with the Marquis.

It would be more than a wonderful experience for her, but he would undoubtedly be bored to have to take a woman with him.

A woman could not travel so fast or so far as a man and she would certainly prefer to sleep in a comfortable bed rather than in a cave or on the side of a mountain.

Lanthia remembered that her mother had often gone abroad with her father, but they had not been to such wild and uninhabited places as he had visited when he was on his own.

She turned away from the window.

'I shall just have to content myself with reading all about what the men have done,' she told herself.

Unexpectedly there was a knock on the door and she wondered who it could be.

Then, with the irresistible hope that it might be the Marquis, she opened the door.

Outside were two young boys, one was a pageboy wearing the livery of *The Langham*.

She was about to ask them what they wanted, when the taller and older boy piped up,

"There's been an accident, miss, to the Marquis of Rakecliffe and he asks you to come to 'im."

"*An accident*!" Lanthia exclaimed in horror to the boys. "Where is he?"

"He be downstairs, miss, in a carriage a-waitin' for you."

"I will come *at once*."

She ran out into the corridor and as the two boys moved quickly in front of her, she closed and locked the door before following them.

They took her down in the lift and then the older of the boys hurried ahead with Lanthia behind him.

She was running as they passed by the porter in the hall without speaking.

She followed the boys through the front door and down the steps and she could see a closed carriage drawn up at the entrance.

As he pulled open the door, Lanthia knew this must be where the Marquis was waiting for her.

By this time it was dusk, but the hotel's electric lights had not yet been switched on at the entrance.

The inside of the carriage was dark, but she could see a man on the back seat.

"What has happened to you?" she asked, her voice quavering.

As the Marquis did not answer, she climbed into the carriage and moved towards him and as she did so the door slammed behind her and the horses started off.

When they drove away from the portico, it became lighter and Lanthia saw to her terror it was not the Marquis who was on the seat beside her, but the *Conté!*

As he reached out to her, she screamed.

She would have screamed again, but he held a thick silk handkerchief in his hands and pulled it harshly over her mouth.

Even as she tried to fend him off, he tied it tightly behind her head.

'*Stop*! Stop!' she wanted to cry, but he had gagged her very effectively and it was impossible to make a sound.

She tried to push him away, but now he produced a thin rope, which he pulled round her so that her arms were fastened to her side.

He was sitting well back on the carriage seat and she was only balanced on the front of it, making it difficult to move and impossible to prevent him from tying the rope round her.

Then he pushed her roughly back into the corner of the carriage and tied her ankles together.

He did everything so quickly that it was difficult to believe it had actually happened and there was nothing she could do to prevent herself from being rendered helpless.

The carriage, driven by only one horse, was moving quickly through the traffic.

Lanthia thought the Conté was not only sinister, but wild and it flashed though her mind that perhaps he was mad.

If he intended to kill her it would not be the work of a man in his right senses.

Now he had made her completely immobile, he sat back in the corner of the carriage.

She could see his face occasionally in the light of the street lamps and there was a grim smile of satisfaction on his thick lips.

She wondered frantically what he was going to do with her and how she could save herself.

It seemed as if escape was impossible.

No one at *The Langham* would know where she had gone and Mrs. Blossom would not find her missing till the morning.

The Marquis would be going out to dinner with his friends at White's and not give her a second thought until tomorrow.

It was then that Lanthia felt a wave of utter despair sweep over her.

She was frightened, desperately frightened.

No one would even discover she was missing until she was dead.

She did not want to die, she wanted to live.

She wanted to be as happy as she had been today when the Marquis had taken her to Marlborough House.

In her mind's eye she could see him smiling at her as he had just before they had arrived. It was as if he was saying without words there was no need to be nervous and that he would look after her.

'Why can I not tell him now what has happened to me?' thought Lanthia. 'If only he was a Knight fighting a ferocious dragon he would save me!'

She now remembered something her brother had once told her.

It was when they were talking about India and how the Indians could often communicate with each other by the power of thought.

"It is absolutely extraordinary," David had told her, "how an Indian two or three hundred miles from his home will know exactly what is happening to his family."

He had related to Lanthia a long story of how one of his men had asked if he could go on leave because his father had died.

"We were up by the North-West Frontier," David said, "and it was quite impossible for him to have received any communication from any other part of India. I thought at first he was just making an excuse to slip off and enjoy himself. Then because he was obviously distressed about his father and speaking with an honesty I could not doubt, I let him go."

"And his father had died?" asked Lanthia.

"Yes, at exactly the time he had told me, over two hundred miles away."

"You must have been astonished."

"It was the first time this had happened to me, but I found that many strange things occur in India which we would call miracles. To the Indians it is just a part of their knowledge of what the Chinese call the *World Beyond the World*."

Lanthia had not forgotten this conversation.

And now it occurred to her that the only thing she could do was to send out her thoughts to the Marquis.

'Help me! *Help me!*' she cried in her heart.

Because it was such a fervent prayer she continued to repeat it over and over again.

They travelled for what seemed a long distance.

When at last the carriage came to a standstill it was almost dark and the gas lights were being lit in the streets.

Yet from the inside of the carriage there appeared to be very few lights where they had stopped.

The Conté had not said one word since he had tied Lanthia up.

His head was turned away from her and he was looking out of the window and Lanthia felt he had been in a hurry to reach their destination.

Now the boy, who had fetched her from her sitting room, climbed down from the box and opened the door.

The Conté climbed down the steps of the carriage and, as Lanthia was wondering what he would do, she heard him say curtly to the boy,

"Shut this door and do not let anyone open it until I return."

"Very good, sir," replied the boy.

It struck Lanthia as somewhat strange that he did not say 'my Lord,' as he would have done to the Marquis.

She started to speculate frantically how she could free herself.

Perhaps she could jump out of the carriage on the other side and if she did so she might be able to run away and hide before the Conté could find her.

She had already tried to move her arms and found it was impossible. She could only kick out her legs and as they were tied together that was no help in setting her free.

'Help me, *help me*!' she cried over and over silently to the Marquis.

She thought that perhaps he was with a beautiful woman and would certainly not be thinking of her.

At the same time she carried on praying, 'help me, *help me*', because there was nothing else she could do.

Then the Conté came back and she heard his voice, harsh and unpleasant, giving someone orders.

Next the carriage door opened and a man looked in.

She had expected it to be the Conté, but this was a stranger.

He put out his arms towards her and she wanted to shrink away from him, but it was impossible to move.

He pulled her off the back seat and picking her up started to walk across the pavement.

It was then that Lanthia could see that they were on the Embankment and she could see the Thames. There were lights reflected onto the river from boats and ships.

Now the man carrying her began to descend down

some steps and Lanthia realised she was being taken onto a boat.

She calculated with horror that the Conté must be spiriting her away from England perhaps to Spain and she would never be able to escape.

She tried to scream in case there was a passer-by on the Embankment who would hear her, but it was still just impossible to make any sound through the thick scarf she was gagged with.

As she was so very light, the man carrying her was having no difficulty in walking down the steps.

When she looked at his dark hair and dark skin, she reckoned that he was another Spaniard and she thought too that he was dressed as a seaman.

It took him a short time to descend the steps and cross a gangplank and then she was on the deck of the ship.

It was not a large ship and she guessed it might be a yacht, doubtless belonging to the Conté.

Quickly, as if he was frightened of being seen, the man carried her below deck.

Lanthia was aware, although she could not see him, that there was another man following behind.

They were now in a narrow passage and one light showed that there were doors opening out of it which she thought must be cabins.

Then the man carrying her stopped.

The man walking behind them she could now see was the Conté and he stepped forward to open one of the doors.

She was now in a small cabin and the man pushed her down rather roughly onto a bunk on one side of it.

Then as he stood back the Conté came to her side.

He was staring at her intently and although the light coming through the open door was dim, she could see an expression of triumph on his face.

He was obviously pleased with what he had set out to achieve.

The man who had been carrying her left the cabin and as she heard his footsteps receding, the Conté sneered,

"I do not suppose your fiancé, as he calls himself, will mourn very deeply for you. There are plenty of other women whom he will attempt to make unfaithful to their husbands and who will be most grateful to me for having disposed of *you!*"

Lanthia wanted to scream, but could still make no sound.

"Make no mistake of it," the Conté continued, "the Marquis *will* suffer for insulting me and if he cries out for mercy as I intend him to do, he will not receive it!"

He snarled the words like an animal.

Then he turned round and stalked out of the cabin slamming the door behind him.

It was then that Lanthia became aware of the sound of the yacht's engines beginning to turn.

She thought also she heard the sound of someone, presumably the Conté, going ashore and she reckoned that it was only a question of minutes before the yacht would begin to move.

She thrashed her head frantically from side to side and tore with her fingers at the soft muslin of her dress, but she was unable to move her arms from above the wrists.

Finally, as she tossed again and again from one side to the other, the silk scarf over her mouth fell under her chin.

For a moment she could not make a sound and then

when she found it was possible to scream, she realised it was too late.

The yacht was already moving.

She was *lost*, lost completely, and no one she loved would ever see her again!

The Conté had said that she was to be disposed of so she would either be drowned at sea or killed in some way when the yacht reached Spain.

Because the idea was so frightening she once again tried in a frenzy to free her arms, but the ropes were too tight and she merely became exhausted by the struggle.

It was then that she was praying fervently to God and the Marquis all at the same time.

If she was to die she could only hope that it would be painless.

And that she would not suffer the agonies she knew the Conté would so delight in inflicting on her before she finally became unconscious.

'Help me, God, *help me* to be brave and please do not let it be very painful.'

The words of her prayers seemed to tumble over themselves.

She felt the yacht gathering speed and knew she was lost.

No one, not even the Marquis could save her now.

*

The Marquis waited impatiently while the pageboy rose from the bench and came towards the porter.

He thought that what he had just been told could not be true, but equally he could never underestimate the hatred of the Conté and his total lack of scruples.

"Now listen, Tommy," the porter was saying. "You

took that young lad upstairs to fetch Miss Grenville and his Lordship wants to know exactly what happened."

"I takes him up, my Lord," explained Tommy, "and when he knocks on the door of Miss Grenville's sittin' room, her opens it."

"And what did she say?"

"Her didn't speak, my Lord. The lad with I says, 'the Marquis of Rakecliffe has had an accident and he asks you to come to him quickly'."

"And then did she say anything?"

"Her says, 'an accident? But where is he?' Then the young lad says, 'he be downstairs in a carriage.' 'I'll come to him at once,' Miss Grenville says."

"And that is what she did?"

"She comes with us just as her were," answered Tommy. "Us goes down in the lift then the lad runs across the hall in front of her. I follows them down the first lot of steps and sees her climb into a carriage. The lad shuts the door and jumps up beside the coachman and them drives off."

Tommy blurted out the last few words so quickly he was almost breathless.

"What sort of carriage was it?" asked the Marquis.

"It be a big Hackney Carriage, my Lord. I knows where it comes from and I've seen the lad who called for Miss Grenville once or twice before."

"I suppose you don't happen know where they were going?" the Marquis questioned him.

"Yes I do, my Lord," said Tommy unexpectedly.

The Marquis stared at him.

"Where was it?"

"I were talking to the lad when us was going up in

125

the lift about trains and he were interested in them the same as I be."

He saw the Marquis was listening intently and went on quickly,

"I says to him when you be free, we'll go up to the station and have a look at them trains. Then he says he would be off at nine o'clock, but they had to go first to the Embankment by Westminster Bridge."

The Marquis had now heard everything he needed to know, so he took a guinea from his pocket and put it into Tommy's hand.

Then without a word to the porter he turned round and ran down the steps.

His carriage had not been moved from the front of the hotel and he called up hoarsely at his coachman,

"The Port of London Authority as quickly as you can. We have been there before and for God's sake hurry."

He jumped into the carriage as the commissionaire closed the door and the horses started off at a fast pace.

The coachman would not have stayed long with the Marquis if he had not known how to hurry his horses when it was really necessary.

He drove with a speed which made passers-by on the pavement look up in surprise and fortunately there was little traffic even in Regent Street now that the shops had closed.

The carriage drew nearer to the river.

The Marquis could only pray that he would be in time to prevent the Conté's yacht, which he was certain was carrying Lanthia away, from travelling too far towards the sea.

He could hardly believe that the Conté would go to such extremes to abduct Lanthia.

Yet that was just what he had done and the Marquis knew how terrified she must be.

'It is all my fault,' he chided himself intensely.

He had been warned several times against having anything to do with the Contessa because of her husband's jealousy.

Now he thought about it, he remembered one of his friends who had been talking about the Conté had said,

"I am told he behaves like a madman where she is concerned and the stories of his jealousy are the chief topic of conversation in Madrid!"

'Why was I such a stupid fool?' the Marquis asked himself.

Once again the Contessa had been a challenge and that was something he had never been able to resist.

Now he knew it was a vital challenge for him to save Lanthia.

He could imagine the terror she must have felt on being snatched away from the hotel and to know that he would not be able to even worry about her disappearance until he called on her before luncheon tomorrow.

It was by the grace of God that he had remembered somewhat belatedly that he wanted to send her flowers and that he had decided to leave them himself at *The Langham* rather than have them sent round in the usual manner from the shop.

He could visualise her dismay and terror at what was happening to her and it was with difficulty he did not order his coachman to go even faster than he was already.

He wished he was driving himself and yet it would only delay them if he climbed up onto the box.

Every minute counted.

As they drove on he remembered the name of the

Conté's yacht and thought that at least was a blessing.

When he had been dancing with the Contessa for the first and only time, he had said to her as they moved over the polished floor,

"You dance like a siren moving over the waves!"

His remark was a compliment to her sinuous body and she did glide in a way that was particularly her own.

The Contessa had laughed.

"Why are you laughing?" enquired the Marquis.

"Because my husband's yacht is called, *La Sirena*, and that is what he often calls me as well."

'*La Sirena*,' the Marquis now muttered to himself. 'It makes matters a little easier, if one can apply that word to anything that is happening at the moment!'

The coachman knew his way to the Port of London Authority.

The Marquis frequently wished to moor his yacht at places that were not allowed to other yacht owners and he had no difficulty in obtaining the permission he needed, as the Officers in charge at the Port of London Authority were considerably impressed by his very modern and up-to-date yacht.

Because he knew it would please the Officers, he had invited them aboard the *Sea Horse*, as his yacht was called, and they had eagerly accepted his invitation.

They had enjoyed seeing all the innovations he had made on the *Sea Horse* and they had ended up drinking his health in champagne.

They told him his yacht was undoubtedly the finest that had ever been seen on the Thames and he knew that now this relationship would stand him in good stead.

It was supremely important he should reach Lanthia as quickly as possible.

He had to save her from being even more terrified than she must be already.

He could imagine nothing more petrifying for any young girl than to be forcibly kidnapped by a fanatical Spaniard and whisked away in his yacht to an unknown destination.

'It is something she will never be able to forget and may affect her whole future,' thought the Marquis.

She had said that she would like to go exploring as he was able to do, and he could imagine that such a terrible experience as she was now suffering would only make her cling to everything familiar.

She might be afraid to venture out of her own front door again.

What was much worse, the Conté might have hurt her physically in some horrible way.

'If he has,' the Marquis told himself grimly, 'I will kill him with my own bare hands!'

There was a little way still to go.

At last they turned down a familiar street and the Marquis was sitting apprehensively on the edge of his seat ready to spring out as soon as they arrived.

Almost before the horses were at a standstill he had flung open the door himself and alighted.

He now ran straight into the Offices of the Port of London Authority and charged straight into the room of the Duty Officer in charge.

He opened the door unannounced.

As the Duty Officer looked up from his desk, the Marquis saw with relief that he was one of the Officers he had met on previous occasions.

"My Lord!" he exclaimed.

"This is an emergency," the Marquis began sharply.

"A young lady has been forcibly abducted against her will and is being carried down the river in a yacht.

"I carry with me now the personal authority of Lord Salisbury, the Secretary of State for Foreign Affairs, for you to arrest this very yacht immediately and search it on suspicion of involvement in white slave traffic and taking stolen goods out of the country!"

As the Officer stared in astonishment, the Marquis continued,

"I suspect it is only a matter of minutes before the yacht passes this point on the river. It is called *La Sirena*."

The urgency with which he had spoken to him and because the Duty Officer knew him so well, action was taken at once.

Two pilot vessels were given their orders and as the Marquis and the Officer stepped on board one of them they moved out into the river.

It was with a feeling of relief that the Marquis had already been told that *La Sirena* had not yet sailed by.

Then as the pilot boat gathered speed, he could see the yacht speeding down the centre of the Thames moving swiftly with the tide.

It was with difficulty that the pilot boat brought the yacht to a standstill.

"What is wrong? Why are you stopping me?" the yacht's Captain shouted from the bridge.

He was speaking in English, but with a pronounced Spanish accent.

The Marquis followed by two Officers boarded the yacht and then began a wordy argument as to whether they had a right to search the yacht and two other Officers came aboard from the second pilot vessel.

The Captain was finally convinced that there was

nothing he could do to prevent the Officers' boarding party from seeing for themselves if there was anything untoward that required their attention.

Because he was so reluctant, it was quite obvious to the Marquis that Lanthia was indeed aboard.

He went first into the Saloon with the Officers, but there was nothing there to attract their attention.

At the same time the Marquis gave orders to two of the other Officers to search in the drawers and cupboards they could find.

Then they went below down the companion way.

It was now that the Marquis walked ahead, opening every cabin door.

One glance told him at once that each cabin was empty until, as he opened the fourth door, he found what he was seeking.

Lanthia had heard a noise outside the cabin door, but she did not scream because she believed it would only have brought one or more of the Spanish crew in to silence her.

She had no wish for them to see her tied up and helpless and to have them staring and gloating at her would be very humiliating.

The door opened.

She thought it was one of the men coming perhaps to check that she had not escaped from her ropes.

Then she saw the Marquis looking in at her.

"*Lanthia*!" he exclaimed in excitement and relief. "Thank God I have found you."

She gave a little cry that he thought was the most moving sound he had ever heard.

"Oh, *you have come* – you have come. I prayed

and prayed that you would hear me – but I thought now we had put to sea it was all hopeless."

"I am here," said the Marquis, "and I want to find out what that devil has done to you."

He walked towards her and as he did so he drew something from his pocket and slipped it into a drawer of what appeared to be a dressing table on the other side of the cabin.

He did it so quickly that Lanthia with her eyes on his face was not aware of what he had done.

When he reached her and saw how she was bound and tied, it made him tighten his lips with anger.

He managed to untie the ropes behind her, and then as she at last began to move her arms, he asked her,

"That swine has not hurt you?"

"I have been so – frightened. He told me I would be disposed of – and I thought they would – drown me!"

She was almost incoherent, but he understood.

"No one will drown you," he told her tenderly, "I will not allow this to happen to you ever again!"

He was undoing the rope round her ankles when the Duty Officer and two others appeared at the door.

"You've found her!"

"I have found her, thank God," replied the Marquis. "She has been tied up by those scoundrels and told she was to be jettisoned, presumably when they were out at sea."

"How dreadful," said the Duty Officer.

"Please now have a good look around this cabin," suggested the Marquis without turning his head.

He was rubbing Lanthia's ankles to bring back her circulation.

The Duty Officer walked to the dressing table at the other side of the cabin and pulled open one of the drawers.

There had been nothing in any of the other cabins they had examined, but now he gave an exclamation.

"There's something here," he called.

The Marquis did not appear to be listening.

"Is that any better?" he asked Lanthia.

"Much – better," she replied. "I am all right – now *you* have come."

She was rubbing her wrists as she was speaking and the Marquis could see that she was very pale.

"I will take you back as soon as possible," he said.

As he rose to his feet the Duty Officer said,

"Look what I've just found, my Lord."

The Marquis looked into the Officer's hand at his very own diamond brooch that he had been carrying in his pocket.

He stared at it in mock amazement.

"Good Heavens! What is on the cover?"

The Officer closed the box.

"That is my family crest!" exclaimed the Marquis. "I thought I recognised that brooch."

"Is it yours?" the Officer enquired.

"It is indeed. It is one of the most important pieces of the Rakecliffe jewellery collection. I expect you know it is famous and of such historic importance that it is second only to the Queen's Crown Jewels."

"I've heard that, my Lord, but I'm afraid that I must keep this brooch for the moment as evidence against the owner of this yacht."

The Marquis looked across the room.

There was only one other Officer present who was looking at Lanthia with curiosity.

"Close the door for a moment," asked the Marquis.

The Officer obeyed him.

Then in a low voice he said to the Duty Officer,

"Lord Salisbury himself would wish you to handle this criminal affair very discreetly and diplomatically. You can easily understand that Her Majesty has, at the moment, no wish to quarrel with Spain and in my opinion the Conté de Vallecas, who owns this yacht, is a lunatic."

He paused to ensure that the Officer was listening before he went on,

"What I believe would be for the best is for you to instruct your staff to say nothing to anyone, especially the press, until you have received further directions from Lord Salisbury."

"Of course I fully understand, my Lord," agreed the Duty Officer, "and that is just what I will do."

"I will inform Lord Salisbury immediately what has occurred and I know he will be as grateful as I am that you have taken such swift action and have been so successful."

"That is what matters," he replied proudly.

He looked at Lanthia.

"Are you now all right, miss?" he asked.

"I am very, very thankful – that you have rescued me," sighed Lanthia.

She sounded rather weak and the Marquis said,

"Now I can leave everything in your capable hands and thank you again more than I can possibly say for your quickness and skill and finally your success."

"It's been a pleasure, my Lord."

The Marquis turned to Lanthia.

"Can you walk? Or shall I carry you?"

"I will be all right – if I can hold on to you."

The Marquis gave her his arm and when they came to the companionway he carried her up it.

At the top he put her down on the deck and realised only the Duty Officer was behind them.

"I think," he suggested, "that this warrants a case of champagne to celebrate and I promise that you shall have it tomorrow morning."

The Duty Officer smiled.

"That will be a great treat, my Lord, and thank you for your generosity."

"The gratitude is all for you," replied the Marquis.

Then he was helping Lanthia off the yacht and onto the pilot boat.

It was a very short distance back to the Offices of the Authority.

Only when they left the boat did Lanthia hold out her hand to the Duty Officer.

"Thank you again very much indeed. I am so very grateful to you for saving me."

"You must thank his Lordship for that."

Lanthia did not answer.

She clung to the Marquis as he guided her to where his carriage was waiting.

He helped her into it and then he gave his orders to the coachman.

"Take me first to Lord Salisbury's house."

"I remember it well, my Lord."

"If his Lordship is not at home we shall have to go to the Foreign Office, but I imagine most people will have gone home at this hour."

The Marquis was speaking more to himself than the coachman and he stepped into the carriage.

As the horses moved off, he put out his arms and pulled Lanthia close to him.

"You are all right now, Lanthia, you are safe and I swear to you that this can never happen to you again."

Even as he spoke, she burst into tears and hid her face against his chest.

CHAPTER SEVEN

Lanthia cried torrentially like a child.

The Marquis pulled her legs onto the seat and held her across him as if she was a baby.

"It's all right," he kept saying gently, "it is all over, it is finished and you are not to upset yourself any more."

It was impossible for her to stop crying.

He continued whispering to her as the carriage now gathered speed.

"You were safe, Lanthia, from the moment I knew where you were and I did hear you calling for me."

She was so surprised that she raised her head from his shoulder.

"You heard me – calling to you?" she asked a little incoherently.

They passed by a street light and the Marquis could see her face.

Her eyes were wide and tears were running down her cheeks.

He pulled her back against him and his lips came down on hers.

He kissed her very gently because he had no wish to upset her more than she had been already.

Then when he felt the softness and innocence of her lips, his kisses became more possessive and demanding.

He felt her quiver against him and he knew that she

was no longer crying.

Without speaking he continued to kiss her until the horses came to a standstill.

He realised that they were now drawn up outside Lord Salisbury's house.

Very gently he lifted Lanthia into the corner of the carriage.

"I will not be longer than I can help," he told her in a voice that was deep and a little unsteady.

He opened the carriage door whilst the coachman was ringing the bell.

As the front door opened, the Marquis walked in, saying to the butler,

"Is his Lordship in? I must speak to him urgently."

The butler, who had seen the Marquis many times and was used to emergencies, replied quietly,

"Will your Lordship please go into the study?"

The Marquis did not have to be shown the way and without waiting for the butler, he strode towards the study, where Lord Salisbury always sat when he was at home.

He did not have to wait more than a few minutes before Lord Salisbury, who must have been in the middle of his dinner, came hurrying in.

"What is it, Rake? What has happened?"

"I am sorry to disturb your Lordship," the Marquis answered, "but this is very important."

Lord Salisbury, a distinguished Minister and one of the most respected Statesmen in the country, indicated a seat to the Marquis and sat down himself.

The Marquis did not waste any time.

He related to the Foreign Secretary the whole story of exactly what had happened from the time he had danced with the Contessa.

He listened intently until the Marquis finished by explaining,

"I told the Duty Officer at the Port Authority that everything must be kept completely secret until such time as he had received instructions from you."

"I can always trust you, Rake, to do the right thing and I know the Prime Minister will be most insistent that there is no scandal."

He paused for a moment before continuing,

"The Conté and the Contessa will be told first thing tomorrow morning to leave the country. If he comes back, he will be arrested on a charge of abduction and theft."

The Marquis smiled.

"I would like my brooch back safely. As you may be aware, it belongs with my family jewels."

"That I can promise you," replied Lord Salisbury.

The Marquis rose to his feet.

"I am sorry to have interrupted you when you must have been having your dinner, but I felt you should know the complete story as soon as I could convey it to you."

"You were quite right, Rake, and I will now set the wheels in motion. Can I offer you a drink?"

"I have Lanthia Grenville outside in the carriage."

"Then of course you must look after her. I expect the poor girl is most upset, but I am sure you will be able to comfort her."

There was a twinkle in Lord Salisbury's eyes.

They left the study and shook hands in the hall and the Marquis hurried outside to his carriage.

Lanthia was waiting for him, but she was no longer crying.

And as the horses drove off again, the Marquis put his arm round her.

"Everything is settled," he told her quietly. "The Conté will be told to leave tomorrow morning and never to set foot in England again!"

"Oh, I am so glad!" cried Lanthia. "That means he can no longer hurt you."

The Marquis considered it very touching that she thought of him rather than herself.

Yet he understood without her saying so, that she was wondering if it was possible for the Conté to learn tonight that she had escaped from his clutches.

While the Marquis was talking with Lord Salisbury, she had been thinking that his kisses were undoubtedly the most wonderful thing that had ever happened to her.

She had never known such a sensation of ecstasy as she had felt at his first kiss.

Then as he had gone on kissing her, she felt as if she was no longer in a world of darkness, fear and terror.

She was enveloped by a blazing light, which could only have come from God.

While she was alone in the carriage, she had been thanking God for saving her and sending the Marquis to her so quickly.

She never thought her prayers would be answered or that she would be able to escape from the terrible death the Conté had intended for her.

'Thank you, *thank you*, God,' she prayed. 'I want to live and I want the Marquis to be safe too.'

She remembered how she had called out to him to save her, feeling that he must hear her cry.

He had told her that he had heard her.

She could hardly believe it was true, yet he had said so.

Now because she felt shy that he had kissed her so passionately, she did not want to ask him any questions.

The Marquis was thinking the same.

He kissed her lips again, but very gently, as if he appreciated that she was very precious and delicate.

It did not take them long to reach *The Langham* as by now there was little traffic in the streets.

As they drew up outside the front door, the Marquis took his arms from around Lanthia and helped her out of the carriage.

"Wait until I send you some instructions," he said to the coachman.

He and Lanthia now walked up the steps and into the hotel and the Marquis guessed that because she was moving quickly with her head down that she did not wish to be seen.

However, the porter saw them and enquired,

"Are you all right, my Lord?"

"It was just a stupid joke that misfired. Please will you send a bottle of Dom Pérignon champagne up to Miss Grenville's sitting room and tell the Head Waiter I want to order dinner."

"Very good, my Lord."

They took the lift to the second floor in silence.

He put his arm round Lanthia as they walked down the corridor and held her to him closely.

He was conscious as they passed Room 200 that a sudden shiver shot through her.

Once again she was afraid.

The Marquis did not say anything, but when they entered her sitting room, he closed the door behind them.

"Go and wash away all your tears," he suggested,

"while I order dinner and you shall have a large glass of champagne as soon as it arrives."

"What about your party tonight?" asked Lanthia.

"They will have to do without me, because I am not going to leave you."

Hc saw the relief in her eyes.

Then as if she was ashamed of her appearance, she disappeared into her bedroom.

The champagne arrived and the Marquis ordered it to be opened.While the waiter was doing so, a clerk from the hotel reception desk knocked on the door.

"What is it?" enquired the Marquis.

"The manager asked me to inform Miss Grenville that the gentleman in the room next door left unexpectedly this evening. It is therefore possible for Mrs. Blossom to move into it as soon as she wishes."

"Thank you," answered the Marquis. "When you go downstairs please ask my coachman to come to this room immediately."

The clerk bowed and left, whilst the Head Waiter arrived with the menu.

The Marquis was ordering the dishes he considered Lanthia would enjoy most, when his coachman came into the sitting room.

The Marquis gave him instructions and he hurried away to carry them out.

In her bedroom Lanthia washed her face and hands, feeling that she was washing away the horror of the tight gag over her mouth and the pressure of the ropes round her wrists.

Then, although she felt it would be rude to keep the Marquis waiting, she took off her plain muslin dress.

In the wardrobe were hanging the two pretty gowns

she had bought that morning just in case the Marquis asked her out to dinner.

'I would like to look pretty for him,' she decided.

It was difficult for her to think straight because she was still reeling from the wonder of his kisses.

They had taken her into a veritable dreamland from which she was frightened she might suddenly awake.

'It is something really wonderful and I shall always remember that magical moment,' she thought.

She looked in the mirror to see if her face had changed from feeling such ecstasy.

She thought that, despite the tears, if she tidied her hair, she would be looking as she would wish the Marquis to see her.

The gown she had chosen was a very soft pink, a colour he had not seen her in before.

When she was ready, she stood in front of the long mirror with her heart beating so violently she was afraid he might be hear it!

'He has kissed me because he was sorry for what I had just suffered and wanted me to stop crying,' she told herself. 'I must not behave like all those other women and try to attract him.'

However she realised that it would be very difficult to walk into the next room and not let her eyes betray her inner feelings.

She knew now that she loved the Marquis and she longed for him to kiss her again.

But she told herself that everything was now back to normal and she must behave as her mother would expect her to do.

She opened the door and as soon as she appeared the Marquis held out a glass of champagne.

"I have waited for you," he said, "so that we can drink to our success together. And what could be more successful than outwitting Satan himself?"

Lanthia laughed as he had meant her to do.

He clinked his glass with hers and as she sipped the champagne, she exclaimed,

"I cannot believe that all this has happened."

"That is just what you must think, Lanthia. It was only a nightmare you have just now woken up from. We are going to enjoy a delicious dinner together this evening and forget that it is unavoidably a little late!"

As he spoke, two waiters arrived with their first course and they sat down at the table that had already been laid for them.

Four candles had been lit and in the centre of the table Lanthia saw a very pretty basket of pink roses.

"What lovely flowers!" she exclaimed, "and they match my gown."

"They are what brought me to *The Langham* on my way out to dinner. As I handed them in I learned that you had been told I had suffered an accident."

"So that is how you saved me," exclaimed Lanthia.

She thought it a strange coincidence that she should have chosen to wear a gown of the same colour as the first flowers the Marquis had given her.

But then everything that was happening to her was strange.

Nothing could be more exciting than having dinner with him alone.

Deliberately and in order to take her mind off her ordeal, the Marquis told her what he knew she had been wanting to hear.

All about his visit to Tibet and how he had visited several old Monasteries, where he had been allowed by an Abbott to see some of the special treasures that had been collected by the monks over the centuries.

The Marquis knew as he spoke that Lanthia was visualising every detail he told her about his journey.

He described a long trek he had undertaken in the North African desert to search for a particular tribe which had not been discovered by any other explorer.

"And you found them?" she asked him in an awed voice.

"I found them, but there were very few tribesmen left and the carvings they created had deteriorated over the years. At the same time my discovery was of considerable interest to the Royal Geographical Society."

"Oh, do tell me more!" begged Lanthia.

They talked on until dinner was finished.

It was then Lanthia remembered that the Marquis would be leaving her and she would be left alone.

She tried not to think that the Conté was still on the same corridor, but yet the thought kept recurring to her.

Perhaps he would learn somehow that his yacht had been apprehended and that she was free.

She would, of course, lock her door and yet because he was so frightening, she felt that a locked door would not prevent him from attacking her if that was what he was still determined to do.

The Marquis could now understand her thoughts and fears.

He waited until the waiters had cleared away the table and they were alone in the sitting room.

"You are not to worry, Lanthia, about being here alone tonight. I am going to stay here and protect you from anything that might happen, although I am almost certain that nothing will."

He saw Lanthia's eyes light up.

"I don't want to put you to any trouble."

"It is no trouble at all. I intended to sleep on the sofa, but while you were in your bedroom the manager sent up to say that the room next door has now been vacated, and Mrs. Blossom can move in whenever she wishes."

"I think perhaps I should go home tomorrow," said Lanthia, a little wistfully.

"I thought that was just what you would wish to do, but the bedroom next door will be more comfortable for me tonight than the sofa!"

Lanthia gave a little cry.

"Of course I would not have allowed you to sleep on the sofa. You could have had my bed, because as I am much smaller I could curl up on the sofa quite easily."

The Marquis smiled.

He knew it had never crossed her mind, as it would any other woman's, that they might share a bed.

She was, he pondered, exactly as she should be – innocent, pure and so totally unlike anyone else he had ever known.

Aloud he said,

"I have already sent for my valet to bring me what I shall require for tonight and my clothes for the morning."

He had been standing and he now sat down beside her on the sofa.

"There is one question I want to ask you, Lanthia."

"What is it?" she enquired.

"Do you think," he began slowly, "that I in any way at all resemble the invisible man who rides with you in the woods and who listens carefully as you do to the goblins digging under the trees and the nymphs and fairies hiding behind them?"

Lanthia stared at him in astonishment.

"How can you say that to me?"

The Marquis put his arms round her.

"I know what you are thinking and I know that is what you have always felt, because it is *exactly* what I felt myself when I was young. I have never told anyone about it, as I thought they would laugh at me."

It was then Lanthia knew that he was the man who had ridden beside her and who had been in all her dreams.

Because she was too shy to say so, she merely hid her face against his shoulder.

"What I am really asking you, my dearest darling," the Marquis said, "is if you will marry me? I want you and I know we shall be very happy if we can explore the world together."

Lanthia stared up at him and he thought no woman could have looked more radiant and ethereal.

At the same time her eyes searched his as if she was unable to believe what she had just heard.

"Are you really asking me," she whispered, "to be your wife? But you said you would *never* marry?"

"I said I would never marry, because I had not met you. I love you as I have never loved anyone in my life and I can tell you quite truthfully I shall never love anyone else. You are all I have ever dreamt about and thought I would never find. That was why I was determined to be a bachelor."

He paused to kiss her gently on the cheek before he continued,

"I think that the more we are together the more we

will find that we think the same, feel the same and *are* the same."

"It cannot be true," cried Lanthia. "I love you, of course, I love you. When you kissed me, I knew it was everything I ever thought a kiss would be like only much more wonderful."

"I will teach you all about love, my precious, and it will be the most exciting and thrilling adventure I have ever undertaken."

Then he pulled her against him and kissed her until her whole body quivered.

Her heart was beating as violently as his.

"I love you, *I love you*," Lanthia whispered.

"That is all I ever want you to hear you say," the Marquis answered, "but I am still afraid in case what you spoke of as *missing* is still missing."

Lanthia hid her face again.

"I know now what was missing," she murmured.

"Tell me, my darling."

"It was love, I realised that after you kissed me, I knew that what I was feeling for you was *love*, but I never believed you would feel love for me."

"Now you know I do?" queried the Marquis.

"It is so wonderful that I am afraid that I may lose it," answered Lanthia.

"You will never do that," he promised.

She moved a little closer to him and said,

"My Papa told me once that Russians love not only with their hearts but with their souls. That I know is the way I love you."

"It is such a good description of what I too feel. Never before has my soul been touched by anything I have felt for any woman. I have found them attractive, exciting, and in some ways I have been infatuated for a short while. But that, my darling, is not what I feel for you. This is all so very, very different."

He was speaking as if he was working it all out for himself.

Then as if he could find no more words to describe what he meant, he kissed her again.

He kissed her tenderly until they were breathless.

Then he said,

"I must send you to bed, my lovely one. You have been through a terrible experience and I do not want you to be tired tomorrow."

Lanthia looked at him questioningly and he said,

"Tomorrow I am going to drive you to the country to tell your father and mother that we love each other and I want to be married at once!"

"*At once!*" exclaimed Lanthia.

"We will be going on a very long honeymoon, my darling and it will be a honeymoon of exploration!"

Lanthia looked excited.

"Where are we going?" she asked, thrilled.

"We are going to explore ourselves first. There is a great deal that I wish to learn about you and I hope there are things you want to know about me. I thought we might start in Greece, where I am certain you will discover much about the Goddesses that you have inherited from them."

"How can you possibly think of anything just so wonderful?" she asked.

"After that, we might go on to Egypt and see if we can solve the many secrets of the Sphinx and if we are still looking for more excitement, I am already intrigued by the mountains of Turkey."

Lanthia put her arms round his neck.

"How can you suggest anything so marvellous and so perfect, because we can do all these travels together?"

"It will be a new experience for you and also for me, because you will be with me all the time. I have a feeling, my darling, you will find out many things I have failed to see in the past, because you live partly in another world which is not visible on the surface, but, as you have just said, is deep down within our souls."

He was speaking with great sincerity.

Because it was so different from what she thought she would ever hear, tears came into Lanthia's eyes as she said,

"I love you, I adore you, I love you, until it is impossible to put into words what I feel. You are exactly the man I have *always* wanted to find, but thought he could never appear in human form, but only as the invisible man I talked to when I was in the woods!"

"And I thought there could never be a human being who was like you," the Marquis told her. "So, my dearest, we have a great deal of exploring to do and, of course, we must one day write a book about everything we have both discovered, to help other people who are not so fortunate as we are to have found each other."

"That would be *wonderful*, absolutely wonderful."

Lanthia gave a little cry before she added,

"This cannot be true! Can it really be happening to me? How could I have guessed when I came to London to buy clothes that all this would happen in just two days?"

"No, not just two days. We have been travelling towards each other for many hundreds, perhaps thousands of years, hoping in each life we should find the one person we were both seeking only to be disappointed."

He kissed her gently and continued,

"Now it has all really happened, we must not waste any more time! I want you as my wife and with me every moment of the day and night for the rest of our lives."

"That is what I want too," sighed Lanthia. "Oh, how marvellous everything is, but I am too happy to put it into words."

The Marquis felt the same, so he just kissed her.

Then, a little later as she was lying in his arms on the sofa, she whispered,

"You do realise, darling, that if we are married and you really love me as you say you do, it will no longer be appropriate for me to call you 'Rake'."

"That is just what I have been, but that life is now all over. I would like you to call me 'Victor', which is one of the names I was christened with and my favourite."

He gave a little smile as he carried on,

"I have indeed been victorious. I have fought many battles in my life, but this one was the most difficult and the most successful!"

Lanthia laughed.

"I think 'Victor' is most appropriate for you. If in Greece I find I resemble a Goddess, you will certainly be one of the Gods!"

"That means we shall be happy forever, my darling, and of course live for ever, if not in this world, then in the next, but together and no longer searching for each other as we have been doing for so many centuries."

"Oh, you understand! *You do understand*!" Lanthia cried. "How can I tell you how marvellous this is? I feel we have already reached Heaven."

He drew her closer still.

"It will be pure Heaven wherever we are, because you are mine and I know as surely, my dearest darling Lanthia, as I know the world is round that you are the most perfect person in it."

Then the Marquis was kissing her again, fervently and passionately.

Kissing her until she felt as if he was carrying her up into the sky and they were touching the stars.

The stars were shining within their hearts as well, evoking an ecstasy which was beyond words and almost beyond thought.

It was the perfect love which came from the soul and which was given to them by God.

It was a love which would never die, but would go on into Eternity forever and ever.